Resurrected

Ronda L. Caudill, PhD

Published by Full Moon Publishing, LLC

Glade Spring, VA

ISBN-13: 978-0692203507
ISBN-10: 0692203508

DEDICATION

This book is dedicated to my wonderful husband who wanted a sequel to Forbidden Fruit.

Resurrected

ACKNOWLEDGMENTS

I want to send out a special thanks to CP Bialois and Jamie White, who edited this book.

Chapter 1

The year was 1897 and it was quickly closing in on the 20ᵗʰ century. It had been nearly a decade since the last Ripper murder and things were relatively quiet in Whitechapel. Inspector Anderson had been promoted to Chief Inspector and had married Victoria Whitman shortly after the "disappearance" of Judge Whitman. Little did he know that when he awoke that morning that things would drastically be different in his world by the end of the day.

Chief Inspector Anderson was sitting at his desk, coming to the bottom of a seemingly endless mound of paper work when a rapid and excited knock sounded at his office door. "Come in," he called out not knowing what he was about to invite into his office and his life.

"Chief Inspector, there has been a ghastly murder. You should really come with us to investigate this morning. I know that you have worked some extremely gruesome cases in the past. We could really benefit from your expertise on this one," Lead Inspector Dorian Archer insisted.

Chief Inspector Anderson raised his head, wearily remembering how badly he disliked working cases in the field, especially gruesome murders. He rubbed his eyes, knowing this couldn't be good. "Very well. Let me retrieve my coat. I will be with you momentarily."

Inspector Archer replied, "Thank you, Sir." He returned to his desk and waited on Chief Inspector Anderson to join him.

Chief Inspector Anderson dropped his pen, ran his fingers through his hair, and thought about it long and hard before he leaned over and pulled out his bottom desk drawer to retrieve his trusty friend. The same trusty friend that he would turn to when reminded of the gruesome Ripper cases he worked long ago. He held the bottle in his left hand and uncorked it with his right hand. The scent was old and familiar. It was hard to witness the things he had. It was hard conducting what was expected of his position.

Chief Inspector Anderson took a long, hard swallow of the rum he kept hidden— tucked away safely and only used on such occasions. He let out a long sigh and re-corked the bottle, then returned the rum to his desk drawer. He slowly walked over and took his coat from the coat tree in the corner and slid first one arm, then the other into the sleeves. Slowly, he retrieved his hat from the top of the coat tree and placed it atop his head. He stood for an eternal minute and then walked over to the door and begrudgingly grasped the doorknob. He slowly opened the door and walked over to Inspector Archer's desk. "Let's get this over with, shall we, Dorian?"

Inspector Archer quickly stood and walked with Chief Inspector Anderson to the door.

"Chief Inspector, I know how badly you dislike working in the field on cases such as these, but I think it's crucial you see the murder scene first hand," Inspector Archer said as he walked out onto the stoop of the police station with Chief Inspector Anderson.

"I'm really not fond of discussing old cases. Hell, I don't even like thinking about those cases."

"The Ripper cases?" Inspector Archer guessed.

"Precisely. Let's go and see what you have for me this morning," Chief Inspector Anderson said as he cut the Ripper conversation short.

The murder scene wasn't far from the police station so the two men walked silently to their destination.

Chief Inspector Anderson gasped as he came upon the corpse of this poor woman. He pulled out his handkerchief and held it over his nose and mouth as he squinted his eyes; the pungent scent was overpowering to the point of being revolting. The other officers gagged and some vomited as Inspector Dorian Archer stood in amazement.

Chief Inspector Anderson had been Dorian Archer's greatest supporter in his appointment of inspector. Chief Inspector Anderson had known Dorian Archer for many years; he had worked many cases with Dorian over the years. The first case was actually the murder of Emma Bronze at Doctor Aleister Wellington's masquerade ball almost ten years earlier. Chief Inspector Anderson had admired the way in which Inspector Archer conducted himself at the crime scene. He ever remained calm no matter what the case— always professional.

This case seemed no different as Inspector Archer

3

conducted himself in the same manner as always as he knelt down and began to examine the body of the ripped and mangled prostitute.

Chief Inspector Anderson's heart sank. This was no doubt the work of Jack the Ripper, but how? He knew it was impossible. He had married the one dubbed Jack the Ripper, Victoria Whitman. He had been with her all night the night before. He knew Victoria could not have done this. She was no longer the person she had been ten years ago— no longer living in fear of Judge Whitman. Victoria had no reason to go back to committing these morbid atrocities.

Undoubtedly this was the work of the Ripper. Everything was the same— the body was methodically cut open from neck to below the navel, internal organs splayed out around the corpse, throat was cut, and in one hand the dead whore grasped a small bunch of grapes. Inspector Archer leaned over and took a deep breath directly above the woman's mouth. He looked up at Chief Inspector Anderson and smiled.

"Wine?" Chief Inspector Anderson asked.

"Yes, indeed," he confidently replied as he pushed himself up with the help of one hand on a knee for leverage. He dusted his hands and the tail of his frock coat as he stood. "Well, it looks like the Ripper is back."

Chief Inspector Anderson felt sick as he thought about his beloved Victoria and was terrified of having the old Ripper cases reopened for investigation. He quickly responded, "Could be a copycat you know."

"What makes you think it's a copycat and not old Jack himself?"

"I'm just saying, we shouldn't be hasty in our assumptions. We don't want to panic the public again. You do recall the fear and terror that ran through the streets of Whitechapel before? Do we really want that again?" Chief Inspector Anderson said as he looked around cautiously.

"I guess you have a point. But don't you think it is all too similar?" Inspector Archer asked.

"I do. However, let's just keep this between you and myself for now until we have examined this case thoroughly and/or until there is another similar case. Shall we?" Chief Inspector Anderson suggested.

"Of course, Chief Inspector. I brought you here to help me with this case. I do value your expertise and insight. I also deeply value your opinion. So there will be no further talk of Jack the Ripper unless it's in the confines of your office."

"Thank you," Chief Inspector Anderson replied.

Chief Inspector Anderson took the lead at that point. "Okay we need a photographer here to take photographs of the corpse and the crime scene. We also need all evidence collected, talk to anyone who may have witnessed something, find out who she was, and find her family and friends for questioning. And get her off of the street as soon as possible for God's sake. We need to get this cleaned up and out of the public eye," he barked at the officers. Chief Inspector Anderson then addressed Inspector Archer, "Archer, I am leaving this investigation to you. Bring me what you have when you acquire anything new of importance. I will be at your disposal."

"Thank you Chief Inspector. I will keep you apprised."

Chief Inspector Anderson turned and hastily made his way back to the station. He could not get back to his office and that bottle in the bottom desk drawer quick enough. Chief Inspector Anderson closed and locked his office door behind him as soon as he stepped into his office. He didn't even bother removing his coat or hat before he fell back into his chair and pulled the spirits from his desk. He uncorked it and drank rapidly. There would be no further work accomplished by Chief Inspector Anderson that day. He hid in his office with his rum the rest of the day and answered the door for no one except a messenger he had called for. When the sun retreated to let the moon have its turn in the sky and everyone else in the station had left for the day, Chief Inspector Anderson unlocked his door and slowly headed home.

Victoria ran to the front door when she heard her husband rustling his keys in the lock. "Darling, where have you been? I have been so worried. There is gossip about a horrid murder in Whitechapel. Is this true?"

Chief Inspector Anderson grabbed Victoria and held her tightly in his arms without speaking a word. Tears flowed as fear took control. "Victoria, we must speak. There has been a murder in Whitechapel— it is eerily similar to the Ripper murders."

Victoria slide from his arms and she collapsed in the floor at his feet. She held her face and cried through her hands, "How can this be? We know this is impossible."

"I know. There is already speculation from Inspector Archer that maybe the Ripper is back. I tried to dispel his speculation, but I don't think he is going to let it go easily. He is convinced."

"But if the Ripper cases are reopened then another

investigation will ensue. What if..." Victoria was trying to continue as Chief Inspector Anderson interrupted.

"Don't worry yet. Just stay calm and don't speak to anyone about this or the Ripper murders. Act uninterested and uniformed. We will get through this," Chief Inspector Anderson said as sat beside his wife and pulled her closely to comfort her.

"There are two people we can turn to," he whispered to his distraught wife.

"Can we really bring Aleister and Lucinda back into all of this?"

"I think we must."

Chapter 2

Ms. Poe rushed to answer the door as the knocking became louder. Opening the door, she was not prepared for what she was about to receive.

"Yes. Can I help you?"

"I am a messenger. I have this note from Chief Inspector Lucian Anderson for Doctor Aleister Wellington. Is Doctor Wellington here?" the messenger asked while holding the note tightly in his hand.

"I'm sorry, he is out at the moment. Can I take the note?" Ms. Poe questioned with some concern in her voice. What could be so important?

"I was instructed to leave this note with either Doctor Wellington, Lucinda Wellington, or Ms. Poe. One of these three only. Are you Lucinda Wellington or Ms. Poe?"

Ms. Poe couldn't help but giggle slightly at the thought that this messenger could even ask if she was Lucinda. "Oh, my dear boy, I wish I were Lucinda. I am but an old lady— I am Ms. Poe." She reached her hand out to receive the note. "May I open it or should I give it to the Wellingtons to open?"

"I was instructed to make sure that one of you three received the note and you should open it immediately. It is urgent. Chief Inspector Anderson would like a response as soon as possible. That is all I am privy to." The messenger released the note to Ms. Poe, tipped his hat, turned and walked way.

Ms. Poe looked at the envelope suspiciously as she closed the door and turned to deliver the note to Lucinda.

"Lucinda," Ms. Poe called out as she walked toward the nursery.

"Yes, Ms. Poe. What is it?" Lucinda responded as she rocked back and forth with her small bundle in her lap.

"Is she asleep?" Ms. Poe asked quietly.

"No. She is just laying here playing. I just like to rock her. What do you have there?" Lucinda asked, noticing the note Ms. Poe was holding.

"I'm not sure. Only that it is from Lucian Anderson," Ms. Poe said as she handed the note to Lucinda and carefully took Elizabeth from her. Lucinda stood and Ms. Poe took a seat in the rocker. "The messenger said it should only be hand delivered to Doctor Wellington, you, or myself. He said that we should open it immediately, but I thought it would be best to let you open it since you were here."

Lucinda opened the note. Lucinda's knees buckled as she read.

My Dearest Friends,

I regretfully send you this message. I had no one else to turn to. I felt it imperative that you were privy to this immediately for it could possibly and will most likely involve you. If your involvement is not imminent I will most definitely need to call upon you to assist myself and Victoria.

Please sit down before you continue reading. There appears to have been another Ripper murder in Whitechapel. Please don't judge hastily. It is not what you think. We must meet to speak of this in private. So please keep this in confidence.

We would like to invite you to an evening meal tomorrow night at our house— 7 PM.

Until tomorrow.

Your Friend,

Lucian Anderson

Lucinda sat upon the floor as terrifying memories from the past flooded her mind and tears filled her eyes. She just starred blankly at the note she held in her hand.

Ms. Poe knew it must have been bad news.

"Lucinda? Lucinda, what is it, girl?"

Lucinda looked up at Ms. Poe. "Can you watch Elizabeth for a while? I must go to Aleister right away."

"You know I will watch after her. You never have to ask," she said as she looked down on the shining face of that beautiful child that was so much like her mother and yet so much like her father.

"Lucinda, what is in that note?" Ms. Poe demanded.

"There has been another Ripper murder."

"Well, that cannot be. We know that is impossible. There must be a mistake."

"I hope so, Ms. Poe. But I need to speak with Aleister and let him know. Lucian seemed distraught in his message." Lucinda choked back the tears and forcibly gained composure. She knew she had to be strong for both Victoria and Lucian.

"Of course. Go to him now. Elizabeth will be just fine."

"Thank you, Ms. Poe."

"It is my pleasure," Ms. Poe smiled.

Lucinda turned and promptly left the room. She descended the stairs so quickly that she appeared to be floating. She made her way directly to the front door where she collected her hat, her coat, and her handbag. Lucinda did not wait for the coachman; she ran straight to the coach and climbed up into the driver's seat, grabbed the reigns, and sped toward town.

When she reached Doctor Wellington's office, she was almost completely out of breath. The receptionist greeted her and informed her that Doctor Wellington was with a patient.

Lucinda quickly responded with, "You must retrieve Aleister now. It is urgent I must speak with him."

"Very well, Mrs. Wellington. Just have a seat." The receptionist turned and disappeared behind a large oak door.

Lucinda sat grasping the note tightly in her hand. She could barely stand the wait. Even though Aleister appeared almost immediately, Lucinda felt as thought she had been waiting for hours.

Aleister dropped to his knees at her feet and took hold of her hands. He could see she was visibly upset.

"Lucinda, what is the matter? Is Elizabeth alright?"

"Yes. It's nothing like that. We need to speak in private."

"Of course. Follow me. We will go to my office." Aleister stood and helped Lucinda up.

He held her around her waist as they walked into his office. He helped her into and chair and closed the door.

"What do you have there?" he asked, noticing the note that she grasped tightly in her hands.

Lucinda handed the note to Aleister. "It is from Lucian Anderson."

"Is he and Victoria alright? Has something happened?"

"Aleister, just read it."

Aleister Wellington slowly opened the crumpled note that was slightly moist from being in Lucinda's hand for so long. As he read, he sat back against his desk. He knew now why his wife had looked shaken.

Aleister rubbed his hand through his hair and then rubbed his face with both hands in frustration and concern. He paced back and forth for a few minutes before asking, "Do you know anything more? Was there just this note? Have you spoken to Victoria?"

"No, Aleister. I know nothing but what was written in that note. I have not seen nor spoken to either Lucian or Victoria in several days. You can't possible think that…"

Lucinda's question trailed off unfinished.

"No. No. I was just wondering— well, I don't know what I was wondering. But I don't think that. Someone has to be mimicking the murders. But who and why?"

Aleister stood momentarily without saying a word. Lucinda could tell that he was considering what to do. Finally, Aleister stood.

"Lucinda, you just wait here. I am going to finish up with this patient and then we will head over to Lucian's office and then I will take you to see Victoria. I don't know about you, but I don't think I can wait for dinner to speak with them."

Before Lucinda could give any response other than to shake her head, Aleister was out the door. Lucinda sat and wrung her hands and picked at her nails. She walked over to the window and swayed as she looked out over London. Her thoughts took her back to the day that Aleister's coachman almost ran her down with the carriage after she had left the Whitman's. She thought about the events leading up to her marriage and the days since. She reminisced about the birth of her daughter only months before. How her life had drastically changed. How grateful she was. But now she had this weight to bear. It was not hers to bear alone but nevertheless, it was a secret that she helped to conceal from the rest of the world.

Aleister reappeared, snapping Lucinda back to her senses. "Shall we?" Aleister reached out his hand to her.

Lucinda took his hand and they made haste to the police station.

"Hello, Inspector Archer," Aleister greeted the first person he came upon.

"Ah, Doctor Wellington. To what do we owe the honor?"

"Oh, this is no police matter. We have actually only come to see our good friend, Chief Inspector Anderson. Is he in per chance?"

"He is— but he isn't accepting anyone. You see we have a peculiar case and Chief Inspector Anderson is assisting."

"Please, if you could just interrupt him momentarily and let him know we are here, I'm certain that he would appreciate our visit." Lucinda pleaded as she batted her eyes like butterfly wings at Inspector Archer. Both Lucinda and Aleister knew that Lucinda could charm the Devil himself.

"Oh, Mrs. Wellington, how could I possibly say no to you— even if this costs me my job. I will inquire." Dorian Archer turned, walked over and knocked on Chief Inspector Anderson's door. He said something inaudible to the door and the door opened abruptly.

"Of course! I have informed everyone here that there are only three people who will always be accepted no matter what— that is my wife and the Wellingtons. Where are they?"

Chief Inspector Anderson looked around, catching eye contact with Aleister. "Ah, my dear friends, please come in." He ushered Aleister and Lucinda into his office and closed the door.

"Please sit," he gestured toward two chairs in front of his desk. "You have received my message?"

"Yes," Aleister replied as he and Lucinda sat.

"You must explain. Victoria? We have so many questions. How could this be?" Aleister stammered.

"Let me explain, dear friend. It is not Victoria. She was home with me during the night of the murder. She is a devoted mother and is inseparable from our son. I can assure you this is someone else— who, I do not know. I am frightened to call it a Ripper murder outside of these doors. I desperately do not desire to have the Ripper case reopened for obvious reasons. I thought you should know because of your association with the Ripper murders. I also thought you might be of assistance— I'm not sure exactly in what capacity yet. To be honest, I really needed someone to talk to that I knew I could trust," Lucian admitted to his friends.

His eyes began to tear and frustration was all too easy to read on his face. It appeared as though he had developed five years worth of age on his face since just the week before when Aleister and Lucinda had seen him last. His hair was tussled and Aleister could tell he had been visiting trusty old spirits.

"Of course Lucian, you know that we will do whatever we can to assist. I can see how you are holding up— not well if I may say. How is Victoria?" Aleister asked.

"Not as well as I. That's one reason I had invited you to have a meal with us this evening. I thought it would do her well to have some trusted company to confide her worries to. Will you come tonight?"

"Of course. We would be delighted," Aleister assured Lucian.

"Who was the victim? When did it occur?" Lucinda asked.

"It was a prostitute, night before last. The way in which she was mutilated and murdered was exact and precise to the Ripper murders. I just don't understand who could be doing this, why, and how they knew such details."

"There were no witnesses?" Lucinda asked.

"Not one who would come forward. It was in a back alley where the ladies of the evening conduct their business, so I'm sure no one saw anything," Lucian explained.

"This is very troubling. Do you think we will all be safe? Do you think someone knows something and is trying to frighten us or may be coming for us next?" Lucinda asked.

"I don't really know what to think. I will just continue my investigation. I will keep you informed," Lucian promised.

"Lucian, my friend, let us know how we may assist. We will see you promptly at 7 PM. Thank you for informing us and thank you for the invitation to dinner." Aleister stood, reached out and shook Lucian's hand.

Lucian shook Aleister's hand and hugged Lucinda. "Thank you both. I will see you tonight. Victoria will be pleased."

Aleister and Lucinda solemnly left the police station. Aleister did not return to work. He knew that Lucinda needed him with her. They headed directly back to the mansion.

Chapter 3

As they approached their beautiful home, Lucinda took wonderment in the home that was hers and Aleister's. She was so thankful that they had finally found a buyer for his mansion and had purchased this place as their home. Lucinda could sleep at night— never hearing the footfalls of an unseen person. She had not once felt as though she were being watched in her new home.

"What holds your thoughts so completely?" Aleister asked as he took hold of her hand.

"I was just thinking about the first time you brought me to your home and how frightened I was there. However, I adore this house. I love this place— our home," Lucinda smiled.

Aleister had a sickening look that befell his face—a look so noticeable that Lucinda felt a strong uneasy feeling when she gazed upon his face.

"Aleister? What is it? Have you realized something?"

"That house. The thing in the house is what caused Victoria to…" Aleister trailed off without finishing his sentence.

"My God, Aleister, do you think?"

"The Necromancer was a doctor. He knew how to kill and mutilate; he did have a hold over Victoria. Maybe someone in that house has succumbed to its influence."

"We should mention this to Lucian and Victoria tonight," Lucinda declared.

"Absolutely," Aleister agreed.

Aleister pulled the carriage around to the front entrance. A footman hurried over to assist Lucinda and Aleister down. Then he took the carriage to the carriage house and tended the horses.

Aleister reached over and put his arm around Lucinda's waist as they approached the door. Aleister reached for the doorknob, but was surprised when it seemingly opened on its own. He smiled as he realized it was Ms. Poe who had been anxiously awaiting their return.

"Oh, Ms. Poe, you gave me a fright," Aleister smiled as he and Lucinda crossed the threshold.

"Doctor Wellington, Lucinda, have you found anything?" Ms. Poe begged.

"Come Ms. Poe, we will explain it over lunch," Aleister Wellington said as he removed his coat and hat, and then helped Lucinda from hers.

The Wellingtons and Ms. Poe made their way to the dinning hall where the servants were already beginning preparations for lunch. There was a massive bouquet of beautiful lilies and orchids in the center of the table. The wine was already on the table waiting to be uncorked. Dishes, silverware, and glasses were set. The brilliant blue and orange flames of the fire were crackling in the fireplace, heating the room to a cozy temperature. The ticking of the pendulum clock at the back of the room between two large windows always gave Lucinda a sense of ease. Walking into this room at that moment made her worries ease as a wave of comfort washed over her.

Aleister pulled a chair out for Lucinda and then for Ms. Poe, then he sat at the head of the table. He rang the bell for service. No sooner had the bell rang than the flood of delicious aroma of lunch tantalized the air in the room.

Lucinda's mouth watered. She had not realized how famished she was until the scent of lunch tickled her olfactory. Suddenly, Lucinda could not wait to eat.

A servant brought in a plate for Aleister, another for Lucinda and then a third for Ms. Poe. As the three began their lunch the inevitable conversation of the note arose.

"Doctor Wellington, may I inquire about the note. You two were so long returning, surely you must know something more," Ms. Poe prodded.

"Ms. Poe, again you ask things that the help should not. Once again I will indulge you because you are more like family than staff. We went to speak with Chief Inspector Lucian Anderson," Aleister Wellington began.

He continued until he had enlightened Ms. Poe to the extent of he and Lucinda. Lunch was long as the three spoke and speculated.

When lunch had concluded Ms. Poe went to check on baby Elizabeth and Aleister and Lucinda took a walk in the gardens.

Lucinda and Aleister walked hand in hand in the gardens. It was if no time had passed at all— as if they were first in love. They came to Lucinda's favorite spot under a massive oak tree that seemed to branch out of a quarter of an acre. Of course, Lucinda knew this was impossible but it did branch out over a large portion of the yard. She so loved the way that the leaves turned beautiful red, golden, and orange colors in the fall. How they fell and made such a colorful carpet that compared to none man made.

Aleister and Lucinda sat upon the ground under that tree. Aleister pulled her closely and whispered in her ear, "There is nothing to fear. I will protect you forever with my life. We do not even know if we should have fear yet. So may I enjoy your company and your full attention for about an hour?"

Lucinda couldn't help but to smile as she let Aleister coax her back into a lying position on the ground. He hovered over and kissed her passionately. He let his hands explore as she began to loose control. She could think of nothing except being there with Aleister and what he was doing to her. His hand found its way to her soft spot that was always welcoming to him. As he moved his fingers her body found the rhythm and was lulled into euphoria.

Lucinda's breathing became frantic and heavy. She took both of her hands and pulled his face to hers and kissed him with great fervor. The intensity of the kisses caused Aleister to grow so hard that he could wait no longer. He quickly removed her undergarments and then exposed and positioned himself to enter. The anticipation always took Lucinda by surprise— how much it enhanced his entrance.

Aleister took what was his and Lucinda gave to him what was his. The rhythmic sway of their bodies made Lucinda deaf and blind to everything else in the world. For that brief period in time she only knew the pleasure of being Aleister's wife.

Chapter 4

Victoria made her way to the door before her favorite servant Marie could. She was excited about seeing her friends Aleister and Lucinda Wellington. She quickly pulled the door open to find her dear friends standing there.

Hugs immediately ensued as Lucinda and Victoria were first to embrace and then Aleister gave a loving, brotherly hug to Victoria. Lucian approached before the Wellingtons had time to make their way across the threshold.

"Ah Lucinda," he said as he hugged her and then shook hands with Aleister. "Please come in." He gestured toward the foyer.

"Thank you so much for coming. This means so much to me," Victoria said as she took Lucinda and Aleister's coats and hats.

Marie came in to help Victoria in accepting her guests as she took the coats and hats and hung them on the intricately carved coat tree by the entrance, allowing Victoria to see her guests into the parlor.

Once in the parlor the four friends sat and discretely discussed the issue at hand, hushing as the servants came and went. Aleister and Lucinda explained their brief thoughts on the house that Aleister had lived in when the Ripper murders had occurred almost a decade ago.

The Andersons were fascinated. And they felt this might give them somewhere to begin regarding the new

Ripper murder.

Marie called the four friends to the dinning hall. "Mr. and Mrs. Anderson, dinner is served."

They enjoyed their meal and one another's company since they felt they had a place to begin their inquiries. The evening passed all too quickly, but alas it was time to depart.

As Lucian and Victoria walked Aleister and Lucinda to the door and gathered their hats and coats Lucian said, "Aleister, thank you so much. Without your help we would have nowhere to begin."

"You are very welcome. You and Victoria have been dear friends for so long. You know we will do whatever we can," Aleister said as he took hold of Lucinda's hand and smiled.

"Yes, of course. Whatever you need," Lucinda chimed in.

The couples bid farewell. Aleister and Lucinda met their coachman on the front lawn and Lucian and Victoria, hand in hand, closed the door.

******

The coachman's gloved hand reached out to Lucinda and then to Doctor Aleister Wellington. Once they were settled into carriage, the coachman flicked the reigns and sped toward the Wellington's home.

Before long, and with very little conversation, they were back to their safe haven. Again Lucinda slid her hand into the white-gloved hand of the coachman after Aleister had made his way from the carriage.

"Aleister, should we have one of your famous masquerade balls and invite the lovely Lady Darlington? We could nonchalantly inquire of her if the house is still to her liking? Maybe she would divulge if anyone in the house is behaving strangely."

"That is a splendid idea. I will send invites to a select few— Lucian and Victoria being amongst them. Lucian would be able to begin his inquiry."

Ms. Poe opened the door before Lucinda and Aleister even reached the beautiful heavy oak door that was inviting to all who came upon it.

"How was your evening? Come in," Ms. Poe said as she ushered the two through the door, taking coats and hats and placing them on the coat tree. "I will have a bath drawn for you both. Miss Elizabeth is already sound asleep."

"Was she any trouble?" Lucinda asked.

"Not at all; she never is." Ms. Poe smiled and hurried off to have the servants prepare a bath.

Lucinda and Aleister made their way to the nursery to check on their little Elizabeth. There she lay, sound asleep and swaddled snuggly. Her rosy cheeks stood out against her flawless snow-white skin. Her beautiful blonde curls wisped around her head uncontrollably. Her tiny eyelids covering her sea green eyes quivered as she dreamed.

"I wonder what she dreams of tonight," Lucinda whispered as she leaned her head against Aleister's chest.

"Probably what annoyingly doting parents she has." Aleister wrapped his arms a round Lucinda's waist as he whispered in her ear.

"I'm certain you are right." Lucinda smiled and sighed.

They each took a turn at delivering the slightest of kisses upon their daughter's tender cheek. They then slipped out of the nursery and closed the door.

"I need to address a few things in my office," Aleister said as he kissed her on the mouth.

Lucinda smiled at receiving such a tender kiss after ten years of being together. "Very well. I will see what the progress is on the bath. I will have you called when it is ready."

Aleister smiled and nodded his head as he descended the stairs and headed toward his office. Lucinda went to the bedroom where she found several maids and Ms. Poe drawing a hot bath.

"Ms. Poe, you work fast." Lucinda smiled, hardly able to believe the rapid progress.

"My dear, I was expecting you early. I knew you couldn't stay away from your little bundle too long. I had the water heated on the stove. It is almost ready. Would you like me to call Doctor Wellington?"

"No, thank you. I will get him myself."

Lucinda hurried down the stairs and into Aleister's office. He sat buried under a mound of papers. Lucinda's mouth dropped open when she read what was upon the papers.

"Aleister! What is all of this?" She picked up a tattered newspaper article with a headline that read *Jack the Ripper Strikes Again.* Her hands trembled.

"I kept everything. I'm not sure why. Even after we knew who it was and the reasons behind the murders, I still felt I should hold them back. I have everything I could get my hands on: the letters from Lucian to Sylvia, the newspaper articles, autopsy reports, even the photographs from the murder scenes. I had an overwhelming desire— a pull if you may— to come in here and to go through some of these things. I had no idea that you would see this. The last thing I desire is to upset you."

Aleister pushed his chair back and stood. He paused for only a brief moment waiting on a reaction from Lucinda. When she began to speak he hurried around his desk to comfort her.

"What good is it to go through this? We know it isn't Victoria," Lucinda declared defensively.

"Do not mistake my actions as being suspicious of Victoria. That is not my intention. I merely thought that this might shed light on the new string of murders."

"You are probably right. But can we put this behind us tonight?"

"Of course." Aleister kissed Lucinda and held her close.

Lucinda enjoyed his embrace and felt as if nothing could ever again harm her as long as she was in his arms. She smiled and looked up at him. "I came to tell you the bath is nearly ready."

"That is something to smile about."

Aleister lead her up the stairs of the dimly lit house to the bedroom. The maids were finishing the bath by splashing a bit of lavender oil in the steaming water. The scent flooded the room with a calm that washed over Lucinda and Aleister.

Lucinda fell asleep almost immediately that night. In her dream she walked down a long alley that she recognized. It was the same disgusting alley she had been forced to spend the night in over ten years ago when she fled Judge Whitman's clutches. Lucinda smelled the stench of feces and urine but she caught the scent of something else— something she could not readily make out. She heard the voices of a man and a woman behind her whispering and giggling. It was the unmistakable voices of a prostitute and her customer.

Lucinda turned just in time to see a shiny steel knife welded by a black-gloved hand thrust into the woman's abdomen with great precision. With one fell swoop, the knife had sliced from its starting point to the prostitute's sternum. The black-gloved hand quickly pulled the knife from the woman's body. The poor prostitute, in a feeble attempt to keep her organs in place, desperately grabbed at her midsection as they began to spill out. With death in her eyes, she gazed pleadingly into Lucinda's. The prostitute then fell to the ground and lay splayed out like a melon dropped from the second story of a building.

Lucinda held her mouth and quietly backed into the shadows hidden from view of the killer as he knelt by the corpse and carved at it like a Halloween pumpkin. Frozen in fear, Lucinda closed her eyes tightly and prayed to be anywhere but there and she immediately woke in a cold sweat.

"Lucinda, are you alright? What is it?" Aleister asked.

Drenched with sweat and tears flowing down her

face, Lucinda responded between sniffles. "It's happening again. Another prostitute has been murdered. It was down the back alley I emerged from the morning we met."

"What are you talking about?" Aleister asked as he tried to wipe away some of the ever-flowing tears.

"I just saw it— in a dream. Just like before."

*****

Victoria and Lucian went to check on their son, Alexander. He slept soundly— not a care in the world. Oh how wonderful to be so innocent, Victoria thought as she reached down and held his tiny soft hand. She leaned over and kissed him. Lucian lightly rested his hand on the top of the baby's head while stroking his forehead with his thumb.

"He will one day be a splendid man— someone we will both be proud of. He is destined to do greatness," Lucian said to Victoria, never looking away from his son.

"I just hope I can be there throughout his journey to manhood," Victoria whispered, the words catching in her throat.

"What do you mean? You know you will be here for him." Lucian reached out with his free hand and grasped Victoria's hand reassuringly.

"Lucian, if this case is reopened... well, you know what could happen."

"There is no evidence and nothing to really tie you to any of the Ripper murders and you definitely have an alibi for this one."

"Yes, and what a believable alibi— sleeping in the bed with my husband."

"That is the honest truth," Lucian tried to be reassuring, but he himself was deeply troubled— not only about the possibility of the Ripper case being reopened, but also who had committed the most recent murder and why.

Night had fallen hours earlier and the evenings were increasingly colder. Lucian and Victoria settled in for what they hoped would be a long night's sleep. Victoria's sleep was not as restful as Lucian's. She tossed and turned, plagued with dreams of what she had done ten years ago to protect Lucinda and rid them forever of her abusive father, Judge Whitman.

Every murder was played out in her unconscious mind, every detail— how she could see everything, every terrible act that was being done by her hands and how it was all involuntary. Whatever had taken up residence in her soul had helped her mind rationalize the murders. The veil was lifted from Victoria's clouded eyes. Once her friends had found her on the back lawn with her bloodied hands gripping the knife that had torn into her father's flesh, leaving him to harm no one else, and they helped to conceal it, could she see clearly how sinister her actions actually were. Victoria awoke that morning filled with regret and dread.

That morning Victoria had risen before her husband. She dressed quietly and made her way to the kitchen where Marie was already preparing a breakfast fit for a king. The scent of the eggs and ham made Victoria's mouth water.

Lucian went to the dining hall for breakfast.

Moments later Victoria joined her husband in the dining hall. She sat and absentmindedly went through the motions of accepting her plate, placing her napkin in her lap and picking up her fork. Victoria was not herself and he could tell.

Lucian had called her name three times before his voice penetrated her thoughts.

"Victoria, are you feeling well? You seem very distracted," Lucian asked.

"I just had dreams about..." she stopped mid sentence as Marie entered the room to bring milk to them. When Marie exited, Victoria began again in a whisper, "about the other murders— before. They were in such detail. I find it very hard at times to live with— well, you know."

Lucian tried to reassure his fragile wife. "Victoria, what is done is done. You weren't yourself then. We all have a hand in it— when we decided to feed that pig to the pigs we all became involved. There is no turning back. You have to control yourself. You have a son now to care for and protect."

He had never seen her this upset and fragile before. She had always been so strong.

Lucian and Victoria quietly finished their breakfast. Lucian bid his wife farewell for the day and kissed her.

Victoria tried to damper her concern by keeping herself busy with Alexander.

Chapter 5

Chief Inspector Anderson walked through the door of the police station to find everything in an uproar as he was immediately greeted by Inspector Dorian Archer.

"Dorian, what is going on?" he questioned as he led Inspector Archer Usher into his office.

"Another prostitute has been found murdered— in an alley."

Chief Inspector Anderson sighed and agitatedly ran his hands through his hair. "Very well. Shall we visit the crime scene?"

"Right away, Sir," Inspector Archer said as he grabbed his hat and frock coat from the coat tree in his office as Chief Inspector Anderson stood silently in the same spot that Inspector Archer had left him.

Inspector Archer was back before Chief Inspector Anderson could even really get a complete thought finished.

"Shall we?" Inspector Archer asked.

"Of course. After you," Chief Inspector Anderson said as he gestured toward the door with his hand.

Inspector Archer stepped out onto the stoop closely followed by Chief Inspector Anderson. The men again walked to the murder scene. As they approached the corpse, several policemen were gagging while others looked away trying not to vomit.

Inspector Archer was horror stricken when he saw the remains of the poor prostitute. Her mangled body lay in a pool of blood while her organs lay strewn about her, spilling from the gapping hole in her torso. The scene was complete with a small bunch of grapes in her left hand and a wine stain on her blouse.

Chief Inspector Anderson had no choice but to declare it a Ripper murder. The similarities were uncanny. Hopefully he could keep Victoria and the Wellingtons out of it.

Inspector Archer and Chief Inspector Anderson knelt by the body for further examination. Chief Inspector Anderson pulled a penknife from his trouser pocket. He opened it and began to probe at the open flesh lined with yellow fat. After several minutes of examination Chief Inspector Anderson stood. He methodically dusted his frock coat and trousers. He pulled his handkerchief from his coat and wiped the penknife blade. Slowly, he closed the knife and returned it to his trousers pocket and looked at Inspector Archer grimly.

"I suppose now is the time to officially link these to the Ripper murders. However, I don't want this to get out to the public. So make certain all of the men understand to not mention the word 'Ripper' to the press," Chief Inspector Anderson instructed Inspector Archer.

"Understood, Chief Inspector." Inspector Archer stood and dusted himself. "I will get the evidence collected and photographs taken, then have the men canvas the area for possible witnesses and take statements. We will get things taken care of here as soon as possible and get the alley cleared."

"Very well." Chief Inspector Anderson headed back

to the police station.

He knew this time he couldn't bury his troubles in his bottle and lock himself away from the world. As soon as he reached the station he pulled the old Ripper files from a dusty old box stored in the basement of the station. He spent the entire evening sifting through the old crumpled papers and photographs.

The beautiful yellows and oranges of sunset fell upon the yellowed paperwork that Chief Inspector Anderson was scrutinizing when he realized that he heard nothing but silence. When he finally pulled his head from his work he found that he was the last one in the station.

Panic filled his heart as he hurried to collect his coat and hat. He hurriedly made his way home. As he had suspected, Victoria met him at the door.

"Lucian! Where have you been? Is it true? Has there been another murder?" Victoria was frantic and shaking.

"Unfortunately, yes. I am afraid we must open the old Ripper case. I have instructed everyone at the station to be discreet— especially with the press. So hopefully we can ascertain whom the murderer is before anyone looks too closely at the old files. At the moment, I am in charge of the old case files. So try not to be too concerned yet. Keep your thoughts and your days occupied with our son. I will protect you both."

Lucian held Victoria closely and tightly. She never wanted to leave his strong, safe arms.

Chapter 6

The young boy hid fearfully in the closet, hoping that he would soon leave. That he would stop the torture and the screaming. The boy's mother cried and pleaded with the man— his father. It was no use. With blow after blow blood from the boy's mother splattered against the closet as the boy secretly watched in terror through the crack of the door.

One last loud blow to his mother was all it took. After receiving a brutal punch to the face she fell back against the dog irons that held blazing logs and red embers in place. All was quiet. His father ran away, realizing what he had done. The police came to find the boy cradling his mother's head in his lap weeping uncontrollably and calling to his mother. "Momma, please wake up, Momma."

The lead inspector gently moved the mother's bloody and battered head from the boy's lap and carefully laid her to the side of the boy. He ushered the child to his feet.

"Come, lad. There is nothing to be done here. I am sorry."

The kind inspector led the boy to a chair in another room.

"Can you tell me what happened?" the inspector asked as he knelt in the floor at the boy's legs so as to be face to face with the child.

"My papa. He would not stop. He just kept hitting

33

her over and over. I hid in the closet. I was so afraid," the boy sniffled, unable to cry any more tears.

"It's alright. You could not have stopped him. He would have done you in as well." The inspector reached up and put a firm reassuring hand on the boy's shoulder. "Do you know where he went?"

"Um, most likely the pub. He is always at the pub." The boy sniffed again as the words caught in his throat.

"What is your name, son?" the inspector asked the traumatized boy.

"Dorian. Dorian Archer, Sir."

Those words echoed throughout Dorian's ears as he awoke with a start. He had not thought nor dreamed of this since he had become a police officer. Why would he have such a terrible realistic dream? Why should he once again be plagued with these memories?

Dorian knew there would be no further sleep that night. He did not relish the thought of pacing until daybreak so he dressed and went to the station. He went into Chief Inspector Anderson's office and began to sift through the mound of papers and photographs that lay splayed across the desk.

After a few hours of close examination he heard the hustle and bustle of the police station coming to life. Soon the door opened and Chief Inspector Anderson stood in the threshold with puzzled look upon his face.

"Inspector, is there a reason you have infiltrated my office?"

"Chief Inspector... I apologize. I just could not

sleep. This case is resting weary upon me. I thought I might find something of use. And if not, I could at least familiarize myself more appropriately with the case in order to better assist you," Inspector Archer responded apologetically.

Chief Inspector Anderson, upon initial discovery of the inspector in his office going through the files, was angry. After only a few moments his anger turned to appreciation. He knew that the inspector was committed to this case.

"Were it anyone else, I would probably have your job for intruding without my permission. However, considering the circumstances, I think we can overlook it this time. Did you find anything of use?"

"Actually, I did find something interesting, maybe a starting point— the Wellingtons. It appears that there was much concern surrounding Lucinda. Was she targeted by the Ripper? Why were there so much interest pertaining to her and her welfare surrounding the murders?"

Chief Inspector Anderson knew that he would have to answer the questions as best he could without incriminating anyone. So he began to recap the events of the Ripper murders and the reason behind the concern of Lucinda. This led to questions about Doctor Wellington, Melinda Whitman, Victoria, the events at Lady Kinsington's, and the disappearance of Judge Whitman.

"What are these other cases that you have here?" Inspector Archer asked as he held up two files— one labeled Emma Bronze murder and one labeled Lady Kinsington's stable manager murder. "I was at the Emma Bronze crime scene if you remember. Was there something special about this murder?"

"Those are murders that I thought were Ripper murders but the Commissioner thought differently. Can I speak candidly and in confidence?"

"Of course."

"I am certain that these cases are connected in some manner, however the royal family wanted these kept separate from the Ripper murders. So they pulled me from the Ripper murder case and put me on these. There was much swept under the rug and kept hush, hush."

"So these were never solved either?"

"Unfortunately, no," Chief Inspector Anderson replied regretfully.

"Maybe we should look into these as well."

"Possibly."

"Can I propose a beginning point?"

"Of course, Inspector. What is your proposal?"

"Could we interview the Wellington and the others? And visit the old crime scene areas?"

"I guess it is as good a starting point as any. When would you like to begin?"

"I would like to start this morning visiting all crime scenes," Inspector Archer suggested.

Chief Inspector Anderson didn't want to appear reluctant even though the dread of reopening these cases was consuming him.

"Very well. We can visit the public areas today and I will send requests to visit the other private residences and interviews out today."

The two men set off to the back alleys of Whitechapel and discussed how the bodies were found, how they had been mutilated and murdered, and witness statements. When all of the public crime scenes had been thoroughly re-investigated, Inspector Archer was almost as familiar with the case as Chief Inspector Anderson. The two men went back to the police station where Chief Inspector Anderson prepared the requests and had a messenger deliver them— all but Victoria's. He thought it would be much better if he told Victoria himself.

Chief Inspector Anderson left early that evening, his reasons were two fold— there was nothing more he could do at the station and he wanted to make up for the time that he had missed with Victoria the past few days.

Victoria was surprised to see her husband home early. Lucian quickly explained about the events in the investigation. They spoke in depth about the way she should conduct herself throughout the interview. He explained to her that the Wellington's, among others, were going to be interviewed again as well.

"We will also be visiting the old crime scenes. That means we now have a purpose for going back into the old Wellington mansion for a look around. We might be able to see if anything there is out of the ordinary."

"Oh, Lucian. This is not good— not good at all. Do I really have to give another interview?"

"Yes, Darling, I am afraid you must. You will do wonderfully. I have faith in you."

Chapter 7

The old mansion was drafty and it was on days like these that Lady Francis Darlington regretted her love of this house. She told anyone who would listen about the ghosts that haunted her mansion. Lady Darlington loved to entertain with séances, palm readings, and tealeaf readings. It was, after all, the latter years of the Victorian era and the age of spiritualism. Lady Darlington was the rage of London in the spiritualist community.

A loud knock came at the door. Lady Darlington rushed to see who her guest was. She was surprised to see a messenger standing there with a sealed envelope in his hand.

"Lady Francis Darlington?"

"Yes. May I help you?"

"I have a note for you from Chief Inspector Anderson. He says that it is urgent you read it," the messenger instructed.

"Yes, of course," she said as she received the note.

The note was a request to visit the home— specifically the kitchen that was the murder scene of Emma Bronze almost ten years earlier. Any other person would be upset in knowing that a murder had been committed in their home. Lady Darlington was no ordinary person. She thrived on the macabre— in fact, she hoped to some day contact the spirit of poor Emma Bronze. The nightly creaks and moans of the house fascinated her. Where a normal person would dread the nights, she welcomed them.

Lady Frances was twenty-seven years old and never married. It was not because she was unattractive. The truth of it was she was an extremely beautiful and sought after woman.

She was also a very independent woman as well as rich. Her parents had both died of consumption when she was seventeen years old leaving her everything— a great deal of money, priceless treasures, and property as well as controlling interest in The Opera of London, which was spectacular and very popular.

The next morning Inspector Archer strolled to Lady Frances Darlington's mansion before going into work. He pulled his list of questions from his jacket pocket and lifted the heavy wrought iron ring that was held in the mouth of a meticulously designed lion. A loud bang, bang, bang rang out in the still morning air as the knocker fell upon the heavy wooden door.

The door opened almost immediately.

"Yes? May I help you?" A beautiful woman answered the door. Her red satin locks were pulled back in wisps of careless curls that danced around her face. Her pine green eyes were shaped like almonds. The early morning sun reflected gently off her milky flawless flesh. The freckles on her face were placed ever so carefully as if God himself had designed and hand painted each one. She spoke in an almost a whisper— very sultry and very seductive in a small, but sensual voice.

Inspector Archer's breath caught in his throat. "I'm, um, I am Inspector Dorian Archer. I have come to look at the murder scene of Emma Bronze."

"Of course, Inspector. Please, come in," Lady Frances said as she stepped back, opening the door wider and gesturing him in with a sweeping motion of her hand and arm. "This way. Follow me."

Poor Inspector Archer could not even speak; he barely got a nod out and smiled sheepishly.

As Lady Frances led Inspector Archer to the kitchen she spoke softly but matter-of-fact. "I don't know if you know everything about the ball that night or not. There are also some things that happened here that was not added in the report. It really had nothing to do with the murder—just interesting information. I will fill you in on all that I know if you would like."

"That would be very helpful and deeply appreciated. Thank you." Inspector Archer finally regained the ability to speak.

Lady Frances began telling the stories as she had heard them. "You see now, Emma Bronze was found dead and badly mutilated right here in this very spot," she said as she pointed to an area in the kitchen floor. "Doctor Wellington's poor maid, Ms. Poe, found her as she was closing the kitchen and dismissing staff."

Inspector Archer responded with a nod, "Huh. Yes we do have that much in the reports. We also know that no suspect was ever found."

"Yes, but did you know that originally they believed that Judge Whitman had something to do with her murder. They were lovers. It was also thought that it might have been Melinda Whitman."

"Yes those facts too are in the reports." The inspector walked around the room looking at the entrances and exits, the dumb waiter and the windows. "You know this house better than I— how easy do think it would have been to come in here, kill Emma, and get back to the ball without being detected missing?"

"Extremely easy. If you want my opinion, anyone that was here that night could have done it. If I were you, I would begin with everyone on that guest list even if you think they are inconsequential."

"Yes, ma'am. I will." Inspector Archer turned to look more closely at the dumb waiter. "Were you on that guest list?"

"Oh, Inspector," she giggled as she put her hand up to her mouth innocently. "I was indeed on that guest list, however, I did not make to the Wellington's ball that night."

"Why is that, Lady Darlington?"

"Well, my parents had just died after a horrific battle with consumption— my father weeks past my mother— of course."

"I am so sorry. I did not know. I mean I was aware that your parents had passed, but I was unaware that it was at that time." He apologized, feeling like a heartless scant.

Many minutes passed before he mustered up the courage to ask another question of Lady Darlington. "Did you know the Wellingtons back then?"

"Well I did know Doctor Wellington, but not Lucinda. I only met her when she began to attend Lady Kingston's School. We were schoolmates. I have known her since— such a lovely woman."

Inspector Archer asked, "May I take a look at the remainder of your lovely home and gardens?"

"Of course. If I can help you with anything, please, do not hesitate to call." Lady Darlington turned to walk but in mid-turn she stopped and looked over her shoulder. "Why have the police the need to reexamine the murder scene of Emma Bronze? Has something of consequence happened? Has there been another murder?"

"I am so sorry, Lady Darlington, I am not at liberty to discuss this case or any other cases outside the police station." He was genuine in his apology. He really wanted to enlighten her. Alas this was not possible.

"I understand," she said as she looked back in front of her and began to walk. "Just call if you need anything," her echo trailed, as she appeared to float away.

Inspector Archer took his time and left no portion of this magnificent home unexamined, but was no wiser than when he had first arrived. As he made his way back to the massive entryway to bid his hostess farewell, he heard her speaking to someone. When he rounded the corner he saw that the front door was open. Lady Darlington was standing in the threshold accepting a note from a messenger.

He approached to thank her as she was tearing away at the envelope. She was startled when he spoke. She had been so involved in her message that she had not noticed his nearing her.

"Oh, my goodness! Inspector, you gave me a small fright. Look. It is so strange." She held the note up and continued. "It is an invite from Doctor and Lucinda Wellington. They are having one of his famous masquerade balls. I believe I should attend." She smiled.

"Well, that is very strange and so coincidental. I think you should attend." He smiled. "I have finished. I shall be off now. Thank you for your hospitality." He bowed his head to her and then continued to the door.

"Inspector?"

"Yes?"

"Well, I know this is sudden and I hope you don't think it inappropriate, but would be like to be my companion? To the ball?"

"Well..." Archer stumbled on his words once again. What was the matter with him? What kind effect did this woman have on him?

"Of course not. I'm sure you have someone of significance. I am so sorry. Please, do not think ill of me." Lady Darlington quickly apologized.

"Oh, no. Currently my significant other is my work. Are you certain that you would like to invite me to be your escort? Surely there must be someone else you would want to escort you."

"No. There is not. You are by far the most interesting, and frankly, attractive man that I have met in many years. But feel free to decline. There will be no ill feelings."

"No. Well, if you are certain. I would love to escort you."

She handed him the invitation. "Very well." Her smile lit his heart. "Meet me here and we will take my carriage to the Wellington's."

Chapter 8

Dorian Archer made his way into work just before lunch. He came in, hung his coat and hat on the coat tree, and mindlessly walked to his desk.

Chief Inspector Anderson noticed the young inspector enter. He pushed his chair back and walked toward Archer when a messenger entered with a note for him.

"Chief Inspector Anderson! I have a message for Chief Inspector Lucian Anderson," The messenger called out.

"I am Anderson." He turned and met the messenger, reached out his hand and accepted the note.

"Thank you."

Chief Inspector Anderson walked toward Inspector Archer as he opened and read his invitation from the Wellingtons.

"Chief Inspector, is everything well?" Inspector Archer asked.

"What? Oh, yes. It is an invitation to the Wellingtons."

"You received an invitation to the masquerade ball as well?"

"Yes. And you?"

"Oh, no. Not me. Lady Darlington received one whilst I was inspecting the mansion. She did invite me to escort her though."

"Well, well Inspector," Chief Inspector Anderson chuckled. "You must have made quite an impression on the fair Lady Darlington."

"Chief Inspector. I think she was just being kind," the inspector replied defensively.

"Oh now, Archer, there is no need to get your knickers in a twist. I only jest. But in all seriousness, she has not been escorted to any function in quite some time. She always goes alone."

He smiled and the young inspector could see that his mentor was being sincere.

"On with business then. Did you discover anything that could help?"

"No, nothing physical. But I did discover that Lady Darlington was invited but did not attend that fateful ball. She met Lucinda at Lady Kinsington's where they attended as schoolmates."

"Well, I thought that was common knowledge. You were unaware of this?"

"Yes. Do you not think is consequential?"

"No." Chief Inspector Anderson said and then continued, "Where do you propose we go from here?"

"I would like to speak with the Wellingtons this afternoon."

"Very well. I will accompany you."

"Are you sure that is wise, considering your close friendship with the Wellingtons?"

"I understand your concern, but I am an officer of the law and I can be objective. I think it might make them more at ease with my presence."

"Of course, Chief Inspector, you are right. Would you join me for lunch?"

"I would enjoy that very much. Thank you." Chief Inspector Anderson turned to walk away and almost immediately pivoted on his heels, "You will thoroughly enjoy the Wellington's masquerade ball. They are pure fantasy— well most of them." He returned to his desk.

*****

After lunch Chief Inspector Anderson and Inspector Archer took a carriage ride to Doctor Wellington's office. The rhythmic sounds of the horse's hooves on the road put Lucian Anderson in somewhat of a trance as his mind wondered back to the day he discovered that his beloved Victoria had committed the murders blamed on Jack the Ripper. He still had a hard time believing that he and the Wellingtons had risked everything to protect her. He did not regret it— not for one minute.

Chief Inspector Anderson was still in a daze as the carriage stopped in front of Doctor Wellington's office.

"Chief Inspector. We are here," Inspector Anderson said as he shook the Chief Inspector back into reality.

"I'm sorry. I was daydreaming about my lovely wife."

"It must be nice to have someone in your life that

you love that much."

"Oh, you have no idea."

Inspector Archer stepped out first with the aid of the coachman's white-gloved hand. Then Chief Inspector Anderson followed behind. The two men walked to the door of the Doctor's office and Chief Inspector Anderson opened the door to be greeted by the receptionist.

Chief Inspector Anderson removed his hat and asked the receptionist if she could let Doctor Wellington know that they needed to speak to him. "Of course. Right away," the young woman in a bright yellow dress replied.

She pushed her chair back, stood, and then headed to the closed door. Her long dress whooshed as the air caught it. It didn't seem that she had been gone long enough to have asked the doctor anything before both she and Doctor Wellington emerged.

"Ah, Chief Inspector Anderson, Inspector Archer how may I help you this fine morning?" Doctor Wellington asked politely.

"May we speak in private?" Inspector Archer asked.

"Of course. This way please."

After they had entered Doctor Wellington's office and were seated the conversation began.

"Well Doctor Wellington, I'm sure you have heard that there have been two murders recently that, well, that are eerily similar to the Ripper murders. Even though the murders are public, we are keeping the similarities to the Ripper case in house. Can we count on your discretion?" Chief Inspector Anderson asked.

"Two murders? I knew of one. When did the other occur? And of course, you can count on my discretion." Doctor Wellington replied.

"Actually the second murder occurred last night. The body of a local prostitute was found in the alley behind the pub behind some crates." Inspector Archer replied.

Chief Inspector Anderson noticed that Doctor Wellington's demeanor immediately changed. He seemed a bit uneasy. He readjusted in his seat a couple of times and seemed to be agitated, like maybe he had an appointment he was fearful of missing. Chief Inspector Anderson tried to keep the conversation calm and rushed through it.

Chief Inspector Anderson and Inspector Archer took turns asking questions about the night of Emma Bronze's murder and the concern that Lucinda had been a target. Doctor Wellington answered the questions matter-of-factly with little elaboration. He knew the best way to be caught up in a partial truth was to elaborate; he was also in a bit of a haste to return home to let Lucinda know of the most recent murder since she had that strange dream.

After he had answered all of the questions the officers had asked, the three stood. Doctor Wellington shook the hands of each and told them if he could be of future help not to hesitate to let him know.

"Oh, and Aleister I received my invitation today. I am looking forward to the ball. I have yet to inform Victoria, but I know she will be very excited. Thank you so much," Chief Inspector Anderson said.

"My pleasure. I hope you and Victoria enjoy yourselves. We are looking forward to it," Doctor Wellington replied.

"Doctor Wellington, I was present when Lady Darlington received hers and she invited me to be her escort. I hope you do not object," Inspector Archer added.

"I did not realize that Lady Darlington was entertaining any gentlemen. But of course, we would love to have you attend," Doctor Wellington replied.

"Oh, I am so sorry you misunderstand. I am not pursuing Lady Darlington; I was at the mansion looking into the murder of Emma Bronze. We are examining the old Ripper case and any cases that could have been a Ripper murder. I am not certain why she asked me to escort her but she is such a lovely woman and I do not know any man who could turn any request of hers down," Inspector Archer said, half defending himself.

"I did not mean to offend. I apologize for being so presumptuous. She is a very lovely lady," Doctor Wellington said. After a short uncomfortable pause, Doctor Wellington continued, "Well, I look forward to seeing you both at the ball. However, if you will excuse me; I have a couple of patients to be seen."

"Of course, Doctor. Thank you for your time," Chief Inspector Anderson said.

The men parted ways; the two policemen returned to their carriage and Doctor Wellington returned to his patients.

"I was hoping that Doctor Wellington could be of more help," Inspector Archer sighed as he hoisted himself up into the carriage and sat in the buttoned leather seat.

"I know. I have spoken to him over the years occasionally about the murders. We have failed to discover anything new. I, too, thought we might be enlightened by something my old friend would remember. Alas, we are exactly where we began. Maybe we will have better luck with Lucinda Wellington. However, it is getting late so I propose we visit her tomorrow. Are you agreeable with that?" Chief Inspector Anderson asked.

"I am in agreement."

*****

Doctor Wellington finished seeing the patients in waiting and did not accept any others. He left hastily and retreated to his home to be with his sweet Lucinda.

When he returned home he found Lucinda in the gardens that she loved so. She was sitting upon the ground hands outstretched. Butterflies of different sizes and colors danced around her as if she were some angel. They lit upon her head, in her hands, and on her lap. Aleister could imagine them taking flight and carrying her to a far away land.

"Lucinda?" he called as if he were asking if it were really her.

The butterflies took flight in a flash, leaving streaks of color in the sky.

"Aleister. What are you doing home early?" she asked as she rose and rushed over to greet him with a loving embrace and a passionate kiss.

"I finished early to be with you. What are you doing out here? How did you get all of those butterflies to grace your presence? Did you dust yourself with apple blossoms?"

"I don't know. It is something that I used to do as a

child. I had forgotten that I could do it until this afternoon. I came out into the gardens to relax and found myself calling to them and before I knew it they were everywhere," she explained.

She noticed right away that Aleister looked amiss.

"Aleister, what is the matter? You look concerned. Has something happened today?"

"Actually, something did happen which is the main reason I came home early."

Aleister continued to explain the visit he had received from Chief Inspector Anderson and Inspector Archer. He explained everything— the questions about Emma Bronze's murder, etc. He also explained that they would probably be visiting her as well.

"Well, Aleister. I guess I will have to explain it all to them once again, won't I?" she said reassuringly. "I will be the first to admit that I was very concerned when this new murder occurred— concerned that Victoria would become the focus of the investigation despite Lucian's best efforts. I know that Lucian will never let any harm befall her."

"Lucinda, there is something more— there has been a second murder. She was found this morning," Aleister confessed.

Lucinda went cold and unsteadily sat back down. "Where was she found?"

Aleister hesitated and stared at his lovely wife— the mother of his beautiful daughter. "Aleister? Where was she found?" she asked, becoming agitated.

Recognizing her tone, Aleister hesitated no longer. "In the back alley behind the pub, behind some crates."

"Aleister, someone knows. Someone is trying to frighten us."

Suddenly Lucinda's strength waned and she was more fearful now than she had been in ten years. Aleister sat beside her to comfort her. He put a loving arm around her and kissed her on the cheek. Amazingly, the butterflies returned and lit upon both Lucinda and Aleister. They couldn't help but laugh. And then all was once again right with the world. They knew the butterflies were a sign of something positive to come.

The next morning Lucinda received two unexpected guests, though she was not surprised as she answered the call of Ms. Poe.

"Good morning, dear Lucian," she said as she received a friendly hug and a kiss on the cheek from her dear friend's husband. "Lucinda, what a pleasure," Chief Inspector Anderson said.

"Inspector Archer, how nice to see you," Lucinda said as she curtseyed to him. "My husband explained to me that you visited him yesterday and would probably wish to speak to me as well. So shall we sit and you can ask me anything you wish?" Lucinda said a she gestured to the coach behind the men and she sat in a chair across from them. "Ms. Poe," Lucinda called out.

Ms. Poe appeared to materialize from nowhere. "Yes, Mrs. Wellington?"

"Would you please bring us some tea?"

"Of course, Ma'am," she said as she curtseyed,

turned, and made her way to the kitchen to retrieve the tea.

Lucinda and the two policemen had already become deep in discussion when Ms. Poe returned with a silver tea set and three dainty porcelain teacups placed upon a silver tray. She quietly placed the tea set on the table and bowed out of the room.

"Thank you, Ms. Poe," Lucinda called out after Ms. Poe as she exited the room.

"Gentlemen, would like cream and sugar with your tea?" Lucinda asked as she poured the steaming hot liquid into the three cups.

Chief Inspector Anderson replied, "Cream please, and three lumps of sugar."

Inspector Archer responded with, "Cream, but no sugar." Lucinda prepared the tea and handed the respective cups to the men. They each responded with, "Thank you." The men continued asking Lucinda questions and she continued to answer. Both Chief Inspector Anderson and Lucinda were very relieved when the visit concluded. They bid farewell and Lucinda went back to the parlor and collapsed on the chair she had spent the last hour in. Ms. Poe entered cautiously.

"Lucinda, have they gone? Is everything alright?" Ms. Poe asked.

"Yes. Thank you. Everything is just fine. I think it went very well," Lucinda sighed.

Chapter 9

Weeks passed and there were no further murders. The night finally arrived for the infamous Wellington masquerade ball. Lucinda had spent the entire day in a hustle and bustle along with Ms. Poe and the rest of the staff in preparation. Guests were arriving and it was time for Aleister and Lucinda to make their grand entrance.

Aleister and Lucinda descended the grand staircase arm in arm, stepping on the red carpet runner like they were royalty. Lucinda's dark green dress flowed gracefully behind each step she took. Lucinda's hair was pulled up but with long ringlets allowed to fall here and there; wisps of hair graced her face like downy feathers. Aleister's mother's emerald necklace hugged Lucinda's throat closely. In Lucinda's free hand, she held the same beautiful jewel encrusted mask that Aleister had given her the night of the first ball.

Aleister was dressed in his black slacks, white shirt, black vest, and black tailcoat. He was carrying his mask—the same one from the first masquerade ball with Lucinda. He was dashing with his dark tussled hair resting above his collar.

When the hosting couple reached the bottom of the stairs, they floated into the ballroom to greet their guests. The musicians were playing and the guests mingling, laughing, and dancing. Among the guests were Lady Darlington, Dorian Archer, Lucian and Victoria Anderson and Sylvia Dalton. There were also other ladies there that Lucinda had met at Lady Kinsington's and had remained friends with over the years; they of course brought their husbands.

After Lucinda had made her rounds, making it a point to speak to every guest there, she eventually broke away from Aleister and went back to speak with Lady Darlington. Lucinda was anxious to speak with her friend Lady Darlington. She knew how much Lady Darlington loved to gossip— if there were anything to know, Lady Darlington would be more than happy to share. Lucinda knew that she would know if the information Lady Darlington shared was accurate of hearsay. Lucinda smiled as she remembered the comment Lady Darlington would make if she was not certain of a truth, "I cannot tell you if this is fact or fiction; this is just what I heard."

"Well, Frances, I am so happy you made it tonight, and with that delicious Inspector Archer, no less," Lucinda smiled slyly and giggled.

"Oh my, dear Lucinda, what are you insinuating?"

"Nothing, really. I just pointed out that he is a very handsome man. You are lucky to be escorted by him tonight. That's all," Lucinda said.

"He is quite attractive. I must say, I have not had a man that handsome on my arm in quite some time. It is refreshing. Maybe I will have a little fun with him but I seriously do not see a long term relationship arising from this," she said as she stared at Dorian Archer.

"Frances Darlington, are you avoiding a relationship with him because of his station in life? Do not forget that I was a lowly maid when Aleister found me," Lucinda scolded.

"Oh no, Lucinda. That is not what I meant. Not at

all," Lady Darlington apologized. "You know me well. When have you ever known me to throw away a good man due to his social status?"

"Well, if not that, what then? You like him, do you not?" Lucinda questioned.

"Of course I do, otherwise he would not be on my arm tonight," Lady Darlington admitted.

"Then why are you so certain that there is no future for you and he?"

"To be honest, I'm not certain of his feelings for me. I don't ever want to experience a broken heart again."

"Is that why you go through men like hats?" Lucinda questioned with sadness in her eyes.

"Can we speak of something else, please?" begged Lady Darlington.

"I'm sorry. I didn't mean to dredge up painful feelings. Of course we can." Lucinda found her opening to direct the conversation where she had wanted it to go. "Oh, I know! Tell me of the mansion. How are the hauntings? I know that fascinated you— your séances, tea-leaf readings, palm readers and table rapping. You know, all of that? So tell what is new at the mansion," Lucinda asked.

Lucinda could tell by the look in her dear friend's eyes that she had struck up a conversation topic that could last all evening. And Lady Darlington took a deep, excited breath and began.

"Oh, Lucinda. We had the best séance two weeks ago. We contacted Doctor Victor Middleton. He is still in that house— still at unrest," Lady Darlington said with great excitement in her voice and her eyes opened wide and brightened.

"Frances, are you fascinated with that crazy doctor? You know it is probably very unsafe— him being a necromancer and all, not to mention the fact that he is dead," Lucinda scolded.

"Oh Lucinda, you sound like a parent scolding me like a child. I am an adult. Now do you want to know what happened?"

"Of course I do. Though I think you should be cautious, I am very fascinated with the spirit world. So what happened?" Lucinda asked.

Lady Darlington dove right in with such enthusiasm. She grabbed Lucinda by the hand and pulled her to two nearby chairs and pulled her to the seat. She held Lucinda's hand.

"I had no friends to participate with me, so I had my servants sit in on the séance instead. It was amazing. We all sat in a circle around the table and held hands. There was my favorite servant Edith, two other women and my butler, Jack. I began to call upon the doctor to come to us, to show himself and to speak to us. It was amazing! The candles dimmed and flickered, then a few of them extinguished on their own. Jack began to shake furiously and uncontrollably. His head fell back and his eyes rolled back in his head— all we could see were the whites of his eyes. Then he raised his head and began to speak, but not in his voice. It was Doctor Middleton's spirit speaking through Jack!" Lady Darlington paused to take a breath.

Lucinda took advantage of this slight pause to ask a question. "So what did he say?"

Lady Darlington took a deep breath and began again. "He spoke with the most sinister, deep voice. It actually sounded as if there were more than one person speaking at once. He said he would once again rise up— he would wreak havoc on all of London. He said he no longer had physical bounds. Then Jack's head fell to the table; he was unconscious. No sooner had his head hit the table than a strong breeze blew through the house and the remaining candles were extinguished— it was pitch black!"

"How is Jack now? Did he remember anything? Did he have any ill effects from the possession?" Lucinda asked.

"Actually, he was quite ill for several days— in fact, bed ridden. However, he claims to not remember anything. He is feeling much better now. Although, he is having some trouble sleeping. He has been roaming the halls at night and a few times he left the house."

"That is odd. Where did he go?" Lucinda questioned.

"That, I am not certain. I just know that it was just before breakfast when he returned on each account," Lady Darlington replied.

"Ah, ladies. I wandered where you were off to— hiding over here in the corner like wall flowers," Aleister said as he approached.

"Oh Aleister, my dear, we aren't hiding. I was just gossiping a bit to your lovely wife," Lady Darlington said as she smiled.

"Well, in that case, I should leave you to it then. I have no desire to hear the local gossip. I know how you ladies love it so, though. On with it then. Just find me when you would like to dance, darling," he said as he leaned over and kissed Lucinda on the cheek.

"I should think we will not be much longer," Lucinda smiled.

'Oh, Aleister. I think I have adequately filled her in on everything. You can have her back now," Lady Darlington said as she affixed her eyes on her escort. "I have other things to attend to." She smiled, stood gracefully and straightened her gown, and then floated toward Dorian Archer who was speaking with Broderick Smith— Judge Broderick Smith, who took Judge Whitman's position after his disappearance.

"Gentleman, I hope I'm not interrupting," Lady Darlington said as she placed her hand on the arm of Dorian Archer.

"Not at all," Dorian said as he reached over with his free hand and placed it affectionately over her hand.

"I was just about to ask the good inspector here about these recent murders," Judge Smith said to Lady Darlington.

He then turned back to Dorian, "Well Dorian, do you have any suspects yet?"

Dorian Archer replied, "Now Judge, you of all people are well aware that I cannot speak openly about ongoing cases."

Lady Darlington's eyebrows rose— she wondered if his visit to her home to investigate a ten-year-old murder had anything to do with these new murders. She could hardly contain herself until she once again had Dorian to herself.

"Well, Archer, I must find my fiancé and I think I should enjoy a dance from her. Let me know if I can help in this investigation that you cannot share," Broderick Smith smiled and gave Dorian a friendly pat on the back and walked out.

"I know you cannot speak about your new case, but can enlighten me just a bit?" Lady Darlington asked Dorian while batting her eyes and giving a slight pout.

"Possibly, what is your inquiry?"

"Is there reason to believe that these new murders could be related to Emma Bronze's murder?" she asked.

Dorian Archer always prided himself on being discrete and professional regarding his work. Even though he would not relinquish information to Lady Frances Darlington at her home, he felt he could confide in her somewhat. "Actually, it has not been confirmed, but we are just looking at the possibility. Please be discrete about this. This is a very sensitive case. You do understand?"

And for the first time in her life, Frances felt no need to gossip about this to anyone. She felt a strong desire to keep this in confidence.

"I know I have a bit of a reputation for gossip, but you have my word I will not speak of this to anyone." She smiled and asked nothing else about it even though she wanted to know everything he knew.

They enjoyed the remainder of the evening filled with dancing and mingling.

"Lucinda, Aleister, how delightful to see you." Sylvia Dalton said as she waltzed over and hugged them both. "Cousin, you look wonderful. Married life seems to agree with you. And Lucinda, you look stunning. How is my little cousin? I would love to see her before I leave— if I may."

"Sylvia, you are too kind. Why don't you stay here tonight and that way you can make a day of it tomorrow with Lucinda and Elizabeth," Aleister suggested.

"Let me consider it. I may just take you up on your offer. Now, Aleister, I must know about these murders. You and Lucian are friends— has he shared anything with you?"

"Sylvia, I really don't know anything about them." Aleister hated lying to his cousin— they were like siblings and he felt so guilty.

"I heard that the police think they may be the work of Jack the Ripper. Can you imagine that— after ten years?"

"Oh, I wouldn't concern myself with gossip if I were you— I don't," Aleister said.

The rest of the night was pleasurable for both hosts and guest. The night went by way too quickly. Aleister and Lucinda bid each and every guest farewell— everyone except Sylvia. She did decide to stay the night.

Chapter 10

Judge Broderick Smith finished a long day swinging the gavel and decided that stopping off at the pub would be a nice way to relax— after all, he had no one to go home to just yet. He had a reputation even though he was engaged to Lady Lilly Meriwether. She was arguably the most beautiful, rich, and influential woman in London. She was petit with large bosoms that she kept held tightly and thrust upward. She had long blond hair that she kept down and in ringlets and her eyes were so blue they looked almost white. Her skin was fair and flawless. Lilly's parents were distant cousins to the queen so the Meriwethers had money and status. Lilly and Broderick had become engaged after only a few months of courting.

Broderick came from a long line of judges so he had money and status as well, though not to compare to the Meriwethers. Broderick, being the strapping young man that he was, was never without the company of a beautiful young lady. He was the youngest judge in London at the tender age of twenty-six. He was extremely handsome with the blackest of eyes and black hair that fell about his collar and graced the skin of his neck. He had a fit and muscular build from riding horses in every second of spare time that he had.

When he arrived at the pub he was greeted with a plethora of young ladies. Broderick sat down, ordered a drink and invited three of these women to accompany him. He bought several drinks for them before they retired to a room upstairs. The night was a blur to Broderick. He awoke in the alley cold and sore from sleeping on the cool ground for most of the night. To his horror, when he shook off the fog from the night before and his eyes focused he realized that one of his lady friends from the night before lay beside him— dead and mutilated. He scrambled to his feet and ran directly to the police station.

Bursting through the doors he called out in a panic, "Inspector Archer! Where is Dorian Archer? Now! I need him, now!"

Everyone there recognized Broderick Smith. One of the officers tried to calm him down. "Judge Smith, calm down. Come and sit. Inspector Archer should be coming in any minute. Is there anything I can help you with?"

"No. I really need Archer."

No sooner had the words escaped his lips than Archer opened the door. Before he could even remove his hat Broderick Smith stood and ran over to him. He grabbed Inspector Archer by the arm and pulled him back toward the door.

"Archer, you must come with me now. It is of utmost importance!"

"What is it?"

Broderick Smith leaned forward and whispered to Inspector Archer, "There has been another murder and I may be implicated. Please come with me— now." The young confident judge stood there pleading with his eyes like a troubled child.

"Where?" Inspector Archer said in a calm, but firm voice.

"This way."

The two men left hastily back toward the alley behind the pub. As they were hurrying to the victim, Inspector Dorian Archer asked a myriad of questions.

"Broderick, how could you possibly be implicated in a murder? We have grown up together been friends since we were six. I have known you all my life. What happened?"

Broderick started from the beginning. "I was in need of some female company to help me wash away the troublesome day I had. I went to the pub for a drink or two and a woman or two— actually three. We had some drinks and the last thing I remember was heading for a room above the pub. Then I awoke here in a haze. When I was able to clear my vision I saw her— one of the women from last night. She was dead and butchered. Dorian, you have to believe me. I did not do this. I know what it looks like, but I would never hurt anyone— let alone a defenseless woman."

"What do you think happened?" Inspector Archer asked, his brows furrowed.

"Honestly, I do not know. Maybe one of the other women can tell us something."

"Do you know these women— their names?" Inspector Archer asked.

"Of course, Dorian. I know their names. I have known all three of them for several years. I can even give you their addresses if you'd like," Broderick offered.

"Yes, that would be very helpful," the inspector said as they rounded the corner of the alley behind the pub.

There she was— throat slashed from ear to ear, her

torso sliced open and organs spilling out on the ground beside her. The air smelled of blood mixed with the usual disgusting scents of feces, urine and garbage.

The inspector once again pulled out his penknife and knelt beside the corpse careful not to get his frock coat in the blood. Judge Broderick Smith began to heave and gag. He had been in such shock and dazed when he awoke earlier that he did not have the senses about him to become sick. Now that things were becoming real and clarity overcame the fog, he could not contain composure. Broderick vomited his diner and every ounce of liquor he had consumed the night before. He turned as quickly as possible but it splashed back as tiny droplets found resting spots on the corpse.

"Broderick, are you all right?" Inspector Archer asked.

"Yes, I think so. Its just I have never really seen something so gruesome before in my life. This morning I just ran, but now standing here being confronted with what is left of a woman I was with just last night— it's hard."

"I know, but pull yourself together."

"What am I to do?" Broderick asked.

"First, I need to have some bobbies come out and collect evidence and the body. I will also begin getting any information from witnesses. Of course, Chief Inspector Anderson will need to be called out as well."

"Will I be placed under arrest?" Broderick asked with tear-filled eyes.

"I do not know. That will be left up to the Chief Inspector. But he is a fair man and he knows you well. Just be honest."

Broderick stood there in his disheveled clothes adorned in specks of vomit and splatters of blood. He stood there waiting on his destiny to be determined. He kept drying tears that came faster than he could wipe them away.

Inspector Archer went in to call for a barmaid to retrieve Chief Inspector Anderson and some policemen from the station. "Tell him it is urgent and he must come right away," Inspector Archer added as the girl hurried toward the door.

The inspector came back out to wait with Broderick. He continued to examine the body and found that she too had been given grapes. There was a small grape stem in her left hand. He could only guess that there was no need for wine since Broderick had bought drinks the night before.

Chief Inspector Anderson returned before the inspector had finished examining the scene.

"Chief Inspector. Thank you for coming so quickly," Archer stood and greeted his superior.

"Another? Who reported it this time?"

"Actually, Judge Broderick Smith reported it just a bit ago," the inspector replied.

Chief Inspector Anderson looked at the judge and at first glance didn't recognize him.

"My goodness, Judge, I thought you to be a homeless chap at first glance. What happened to you? Are you involved some way? Have you fought off an attacker?"

"No, Chief Inspector. I have not fought off an attacker and I am involved in a way," he admitted.

"I think you need to explain before we are over run by bobbies and on lookers," Chief Inspector Anderson said.

Broderick began to recount what he could remember. Chief Inspector Anderson had known Broderick for many years. He knew his reputation with women but could not believe he could be involved in a murder—especially one that is most likely connected with other such murders.

When Broderick had finished he sat on the ground and simply asked, "Now what?"

Chief Inspector Anderson responded sympathetically, "You will have to give a statement but we will not hold you. We will also do our best to keep this incident quiet until we can verify your alibis for the other murders. We will also need to speak with the other two women. Maybe they can shed some light on what happened last night. Where might they be?"

"They should be in the room we were headed to last night— a room above the pub. You can ask the barkeep if they are still there. If not, I can give you their address. They all live together."

Then Chief Inspector Anderson asked the two men to join him. He asked the barkeep which room the four rented for the night and he instructed Broderick to wait at a table for them. Chief Inspector Anderson and Inspector Archer hurried up to the room and knocked on the door. There was no answer after several knocks so Inspector Archer burst open the door splintering the wood on the door facing in the process.

They could not believe what they saw. The other two women were mutilated as well. Body parts were strewn about the room so one could not distinguish which body parts belonged to which woman. Blood covered both the ceiling and floor, all four walls, the back of the door, the bed— everything in the room.

"What in the bloody Hell!" Chief Inspector Anderson exclaimed.

Inspector Archer was speechless for almost two full minutes. He just looked around the room in utter horror. Finally, he regained his ability to speak. "Chief Inspector, you know Broderick, do you think he is actually capable of such a thing?"

"Of course not. And he had hardly any blood on him at all. Had he carried this out he would be covered in blood. However, by his own admission, he was the last to be seen with the women. He did wake up beside a corpse."

"But that's just it— why admit to these things and then report the murder and lead us back to a room with two other victims. It makes no sense. What do you propose?"

"I will have to consult the Chief Superintendent. I cannot make this decision; I do not have the authority. We will do our best to keep this as quiet as possible, but there are so many witnesses to Broderick being here drinking and gallivanting around with these women."

"I will send some men up to collect evidence and I will inform Broderick of what was discovered. Do you want me to escort him to the station until you contact the commissioner?"

"Yes, thank you. Could you also have a messenger sent to my wife and let her know I will be late getting home this evening— very late?" Chief Inspector Anderson asked, eyes never looking at the inspector. He kept his eyes scanning the room for any clues.

"Of course."

"Thank you," Chief Inspector Anderson said.

Inspector Archer went back to Broderick with a grim look on his face.

Broderick knew something was amiss when he saw his friend walking his way with his shoulders slumped and the apologetic look he was carrying in his eyes.

"What is it? Did they say I became mad? Did they say I did this? Tell me, Dorian."

"No. Nothing like that." The inspector said quietly. He cleared his throat and continued. "Broderick, they are dead and mutilated. The room is a horrific mess."

Broderick almost collapsed. Archer grabbed hold of him as he began to slide from his chair.

"This is no time to fall apart. You must gain composure. We must go to the station and get your account in writing."

"Will I be held?" Broderick stuttered as the inspector helped him to his feet.

"I hope only for a bit. Chief Inspector Anderson is going to speak with the Commissioner. He said he would have to leave that decision to the Commissioner due to the magnitude. The Chief Inspector will do his best to help you however he can. He does not believe that you are the culprit."

"Who would do this? Why?" Broderick questioned.

"I'm not certain. Would anyone have a reason to frame you for murder— several murders? Have you been threatened recently?"

"No. I can't think of anyone. But I am a judge. I have sentenced many criminals."

"If you can think of anyone let me know. Any small detail may be significant. I really need to get you to the station. Are you steady on your feet?"

"Yes. Yes, of course."

The two men walked slowly back to the police station. Neither felt the need to speak. They both took solace in the silence. They returned to the station. Inspector Archer led Judge Smith into a small room with a table and four chairs. There was a gas lamp adorning the wall, giving off dim light, illuminating the small windowless room. The men sat and the inspector reached over and pulled the paper and quill pen and ink well that was sitting on the table over to him. He dipped the quill pen in the ink well and waited on Broderick to recant the events of the evening before as best he could remember.

The inspector lay the quill pen down and picked up the paper. "I will place this on the Chief Inspector's desk. I will not be long. Would like some water? Or maybe something stronger?"

"No— no, thank you."

Just as the inspector stood and pushed his chair back, they heard the sound of a woman in a loud voice demanding to see Broderick.

"Where is he? I demand to see him now! Do you know who I am?"

One of the policemen tried to calm her down by telling her he would help her but she would have to calm down and be patient. Inspector Archer opened the door of the little room he and Broderick were in and stepped out to intervene.

"Lilly. Please calm yourself. Broderick is fine. Come this way." The inspector motioned her into the little room.

Lilly Meriwether promptly waltzed into the room and over to her fiancé. She slapped him hard across the face. "Are you alright? Am I going to loose you?" She fell into his arms and began to cry.

"I will give you a few moments. We can do nothing further here until the Chief Inspector makes it back. Let me know if you need anything," the inspector said as he walked out and closed the door behind him, heading to take care of a promise he had made to the Chief Inspector— to send a message to Victoria Anderson.

Broderick held her tight. "I am so sorry Lilly. I should have not been at the pub— I should not have been with those women. Can you ever forgive me?"

"Broderick, I am no stupid woman, I am no naive woman and I know exactly what you have been doing in your spare time. I said nothing because I had decided that the day of our wedding this behavior was going to cease," she sobbed on his shoulder— on his dirty frock coat.

Broderick was speechless to know that this woman was going to marry him even though she was privy to his scandalous behavior.

"When will they release you? Are they going to charge you? Surely they know that you are incapable of doing such a thing," she continued to sob.

"I do not know— not until Chief Inspector Anderson returns."

They sat together for several hours. They were in the little room so long that everyone in the station had almost forgotten they were there.

*****

Chief Inspector Anderson finished his work with the case and went directly to see the commissioner. He slowly lifted the heavy wrought iron doorknocker and slammed it against the door of the commissioner's house three times. He was greeted by the butler.

"Chief Inspector Anderson, come in. I suppose you need to speak with the commissioner?"

"Yes, please. Is he occupied at the moment? It is quite urgent."

"I believe he is available. I will let him know you are here. Please have a seat," the butler said as he reached for the Chief Inspector's hat and coat.

He hung the hat and coat up and went to the commissioner's study.

Almost immediately the commissioner came out. "Chief Inspector Anderson. I would say what a pleasant surprise, but the news of the most recent murders has preceded you so it is no surprise to see you. How can I assist?"

"Have you heard who has been implicated in the

murders that occurred last night?"

"No, that news has not founds its way here yet. Who was it?"

"Judge Broderick Smith," Chief Inspector Anderson replied.

"What? That is preposterous. There must be a mistake," the commissioner demanded.

Chief Inspector Anderson explained the entire sordid event. The commissioner was silent; he paced back and forth. He wrung his hands in concern. He ran his hands through this hair before responding to the information that Chief Inspector Anderson had just given him.

"Well, this is a predicament. You know Broderick is from a prominent and influential family— a long line of wealthy judges. And as if that weren't enough, he is engaged to— well, you know. Take his account on the incident and release him. We will treat him as a witness and not a suspect— yet."

"I thought as much. I know this was a decision to be made by you. We have taken his account and he is awaiting your decision at the police station."

"By all means, go quickly and get him released as soon as possible before there is trouble from his family and hers," the commissioner instructed.

"As you wish, Sir," Chief Inspector Anderson said and took his leave.

Chief Inspector Anderson hurried back to the station. He found and informed Inspector Archer of the commissioner's instructions. They went to the little room together where Broderick and Lilly were sitting hand in hand and side by side, regret covered Broderick's face and pain and worry covered Lilly's.

"Broderick, I have spoken to the commissioner and we are in agreement; we will be treating you as a witness rather than a suspect— for now," Chief Inspector Anderson explained.

The couple embraced one another in relief. Broderick stood and shook the hands of both the Chief Inspector and the Inspector.

"Thank you so much. I assure you, I did not murder those women. My only crime was betraying my fiancé."

"Thank you so much, Chief Inspector, Inspector," Lilly said. "If Broderick is free to leave, then we will be leaving. It has been a long day for us both."

"Of course, Miss Meriwether, he is free to leave. I am very sorry for having to detain him so long. I hope you understand," Chief Inspector Anderson apologized.

"We understand. We know how it must look. Please let me know if I can be of further help," Broderick directed his statement to both men.

He and Lilly went to his house where Lilly stayed with him that night.

Chapter 11

When Lucian Anderson returned home to Victoria, he found her fast asleep in their bed with their baby boy lying beside her. It warmed his heart to see mother and child cuddled up together.

He slid his boots off, and then removed his clothes that had been his companion throughout the miserable day that had just faded into a new one. He put on his nightshirt and climbed into bed as close as to his lovely angel as he possibly could. He closed his eyes and quickly drifted off to sleep..

The images of the corpses ran deep. He had seen so much violence throughout his career, but that day had been far worse. He had kept it together well that day, being an officer of the law and not letting his thoughts consider those corpses as women— just things. However, now he was home with his Victoria and his son, he trembled at the thought that Victoria should ever be one of those women. He held her tightly and slumbered restlessly until the cock's crow.

He slowly and quietly arose, careful not to arouse Victoria or their beautiful boy. He went to the kitchen for a drink of water and some solitude before the bombardment of voices, questions, and demands began. He sat at the table with his glass of water in front of him when Victoria crept up behind him. She slid her arms around him and held him closely. Her soft lips brushed up against his face and lightly kissed him, then whispered in his ear. "Good morning, my love. I love you. I know your day was a challenge and your night was restless. Would you like to talk about it? I am here to listen."

Lucian smiled as he turned to embrace his wife and pull her to his lap where he embraced her. "Well, I do not think we have to worry about any of us being found out due to the murders from night before last."

"What do you mean? What happened exactly?"

"Judge Broderick Smith woke up beside one corpse, and the other two had been with him the night before," Lucian explained.

"Did he do it?"

"I think it is highly unlikely, however it does not look well. We are treating him as a witness rather than a suspect at this point in time— per instructions of the commissioner. If no further murders occur this entire matter may well be swept under the rug in order to protect Broderick. The commissioner wants no trouble from Broderick's family or from Lilly Meriwether's family."

"Well then, this is a positive turn of events. Isn't it?" Victoria asked.

"Yes, I suppose. It's just that…" he trailed off. With sadness in his eyes he continued. "They were not like the others. They were far worse and there were three. It's very disconcerting."

"Of course. I should have been more sympathetic."

Lucian looked deeply into Victoria's eyes and wondered how this wonderful, sweet woman could have ever committed murders and mutilations similar to these only ten years prior. It was very hard to believe that she was ever capable.

Lucian decided that he had put in enough time the day before for three days worth of work, so he decided to spend it with Victoria and their son.

*****

It did not take long for the word of the most recent murders to spread throughout London and it made its way to Doctor Aleister Wellington and Lucinda. They were surprised to hear that Judge Smith had found the bodies. They were, however, not surprised to hear where he found them nor why he was there. They, like everyone else in London, were well aware of his sordid reputation. Just a few days after the murders at the pub, Aleister and Lucinda sat before their breakfast discussing the murders and speculation arose to a possible involvement of Judge Smith, however remote. It was not long before the discussion took a turn and they began discussing Lady Darlington and the possibility that the murderer could be someone from the old mansion.

"Frances did say that they had a séance and had contacted the necromancer's, Doctor Middleton's, spirit. I am convinced that something evil in that house has once again escaped, especially with Frances' practice of spiritualism in that house," Lucinda declared.

"This may be a possibility. I know that there is something there— something evil. You did say that she told you her servant, Jack, became temporarily possessed, didn't you? I just do not know what to think. I was terribly surprised ten years ago to discover that Victoria had been the one who committed all of those murders and what had prompted her actions. I guess it could be anyone. I just cannot understand why and why now," Aleister said.

"Well, I think I shall give her visit today. As badly as I hate going back to that house, my curiosity compels me to do so. I think I shall go at tea time and surprise her," Lucinda said.

"Lucinda, please be careful at that house. I remember how frightening it was for you. I also remember how happy you were to finally leave it."

"I will, my love. I must see for myself if there is any possibility of that thing escaping."

"Very well. I know what a willful woman you are," Aleister smiled as he squeezed her hand.

He stood and walked over to kiss her gently on the cheek. "I must go to work now and tend to the sick in London." He smiled. "I love you, Lucinda Wellington."

"I love you, Aleister."

Lucinda sat there for a while dreading returning to that house, if only for a short visit. Her determination forced her to finally stand. She called for Ms. Poe as she walked through her warm and inviting mansion.

"Ms. Poe."

Ms. Poe hurried into the hallway in response to Lucinda's call.

"Yes, Lucinda. What is it, dear? Is everything alright?" Ms. Poe asked.

"Oh, yes. I am so sorry. I did not mean to cause you concern. I am going to visit Lady Darlington today. Would you care to tend to Elizabeth's needs while I am away?"

"Of course, I do not care to mind over her.

However, do you really think that it is a good idea to go back to that house?" Ms. Poe questioned.

"Probably not. This is a task that I do not look forward to in the least. I will not be long there. I just feel the need to see if there is anything out of sorts there," Lucinda confessed.

In a short time Lucinda had readied herself and was ready to leave. She went to the nursery to let Ms. Poe know that she was leaving. She bid Ms. Poe farewell and kissed her sweet baby on the forehead. She descended the stairs and went out to find the carriage and coachman awaiting her.

"Where to Mrs. Wellington?" the coachman asked as his outstretched white-gloved hand helped Lucinda into the carriage.

"To Lady Frances Darlington's mansion, please," she politely responded.

He was surprised to hear her request. He had been the coachman who had almost run Lucinda over almost ten years ago. He had been with Doctor Wellington for almost twenty years. He was well aware of the trouble and the fear that came from that house concerning Lucinda.

"Lady Darlington's mansion? Your and Doctor Wellington's pervious residence?" he questioned with concern.

Lucinda smiled and replied, "Yes. Your ears have not deceived you. And I assure you my senses have not taken leave of me. If this were something I did not feel compelled to do, I can promise I would not step foot back in that place. This is a necessity. On now, please."

The coachman carried out her command and drove the carriage toward Lady Darlington's mansion. Lucinda sat in the carriage and pondered over reasons she had avoided the mansion since she had moved to her new house. Her thoughts took her back to her first fright filled nights and Aleister's odd behavior and strange request to stay sequestered in her room until dawn. Her thoughts kept her company on the ride and it seemed like she was at her destination long before she should have been. Nevertheless, she was there. And it was time to leave the safety of her carriage to confront something she had avoided for so long.

With the help of the coachman, she disembarked her carriage and reluctantly walked to the front door. She paused and looked back at the coachman.

He smiled kindly at her and asked, "Are you certain about this, Ma'am? I can help you back into the carriage and take you back home now if that is your wish."

"No, thank you. This is something that must be done," she responded.

He looked at her with bewilderment. Why had she requested to come here after being adamant about moving and not returning for ten years? Why stand and look at the door, hesitant about knocking?

Lucinda reached up and took hold of the ring on the doorknocker and deliberately grasped it. She lifted it slowly and pulled it down hard to bang on the cast iron base. It rang out loudly. It made her jump with a start almost as if someone else had been the one to release the ring of the doorknocker.

Almost instantly a servant came to answer the front door. A very young timid looking girl asked, "May I help you?"

"Yes, please. I am Lucinda Wellington to see Lady Darlington. Might she be receiving visitors?"

The servant recognized Lucinda's name, and knowing that she was a close friend of her employer, she quickly ushered Lucinda in and took her coat, hat, and gloves. She guided Lucinda into the parlor to wait until Lady Darlington was summoned.

Lucinda had a terrible chill come over her as she sat in the parlor alone, reminiscing of the days gone by when she was the lady of this house. She knew she was being watched by unseen eyes. She desperately wanted her good friend to join her. After a short time Lady Darlington bound in and headed straight for Lucinda. Lucinda stood to receive a hug from her dear friend.

"Oh, Lucinda what a pleasant surprise. What brings you here? I thought you hated my home. After all Aleister sold it to me for so little just to get you out. Do not misunderstand, I am thrilled to see you. I am just surprised."

"I felt compelled to visit you. I felt like a terrible friend to have never visited you in your home. And you piqued my curiosity when you told me of your séance. I had to come and see if he was still here. I guess you could say I have a morbid sense of curiosity."

"And?" Frances asked.

"And, what?" Lucinda questioned.

"Well can you feel him?"

"I feel something— something unnerving. I suppose it is likely to be him— the necromancer," Lucinda admitted.

Lucinda and Frances had tea and caught up. Frances asked Lucinda about her daughter and Aleister. Lucinda asked about Dorian Archer, which sparked a very lengthy conversation.

"I have not seen him since the ball. I fear he only escorted me out of a sense of duty— or only to be a gentleman. I fear I will not see him again unless it has to do with that ridiculous investigation. I do not understand why the police are concerned with a ten-year-old murder anyway."

"So, you really like him?" Lucinda asked.

"Yes. I have never given any man a second thought. I could always either enjoy their company if they wish to give it, or not bother to care if they do not wish to give their company to me. But I very much desire to please Mr. Dorian Archer. I would very much enjoy spending time with him. I greatly desire him to call up on me again," Frances admitted.

Lucinda was taken aback by her friend's admission. She had never known Frances to desire a man so profoundly, nor had ever heard Frances admit to being enchanted by a man before.

"Well, my dear friend, I am certain that he has just been otherwise occupied by this rash of murders. You did hear that there had been three more— all in one night?" Lucinda asked.

"Yes. I had heard. It is terrible news. And I suppose you could have a point. Murder should take precedence over a possible budding love affair."

"I have a splendid idea. I should have a small dinner party just for us, you and Mr. Archer and the Andersons.

You and Victoria are still close. It would so much fun," Lucinda suggested.

"That does sound like such a good time. Victoria and I are close, however, I feel that I never really get to see her or you. You two have your husbands and children. You have so much more in common. I would like to see more of both of you."

"Very well. It is set. I will let Aleister know of our plans and send invites to everyone," Lucinda said enthusiastically even though her dear friend's house made her very uncomfortable.

The ladies had tea in the gardens— the gardens that Lucinda had enjoyed when living there. Lucinda was distracted by a male servant who appeared to be talking to himself.

"Frances, who is that over there tending your roses?" Lucinda asked.

"That is Jack, the servant I told you had been temporarily taken over by the necromancer. Why do you ask?" Frances replied as she looked at Jack.

"Well, he just seems to be acting a bit out of sorts. Is he talking to himself?"

"It would not surprise me in the least. He does behave strangely at times," Frances replied.

Frances called out to her servant, "Jack. Who are you speaking with, pray tell?"

"Excuse me, Lady?" he called back to her.

"Have you lost your senses? Who are you speaking with? It appeared to me that you were conversing with someone, but I see no one with you. So with whom were you speaking?" Lady Frances asked again.

"Well, do you not see her? This little girl here? She said she was a guest of yours. I have seen her with you for the past two days. She asked if she could watch me while you had company because she could not be part of adult conversation," he responded, puzzled.

The two women looked at one another, puzzled and frightened. They then looked at Jack with questioning eyes.

"Jack, we have seen no child at all there with you. Why, pray tell, would I have a child in this house? You know I don't want children in this house. It is not a safe place for them," Frances said.

"I do not ever remember children visiting before in all the years that I have been here. But I did not know the reason behind the absence of child visitors," Jack replied. "But I swear to you the child is standing here with us."

"Jack, maybe you should go in and rest. I will call for a physician and I will call for my spiritualist," Lady Frances said as she stood and walked over to him. She took him lightly by the arm and led him into the house. Jack looked back to the place he had been working as they walked to the house. Lucinda accompanied them. She handed him off to another servant and instructed her to get him into bed.

Lucinda did not doubt Jack's claim; this is what was so frightening to her. Lady Frances sent an urgent message to the Doctor Wellington to come and check on Jack. She also sent an urgent message to the spiritualist to come as quickly as possible.

The two women sat in the atrium— one of the few

rooms that Lucinda felt remotely safe in. They discussed Jack's claim of seeing and speaking to this child they had not seen.

"Lucinda, did you ever see a little girl when you lived here?" Frances questioned.

"No. Never a little girl, only the shadowy figure. I did hear walking and scratching sounds. I never heard nor saw anything indicating the presence of a child spirit here. Do you think Jack really saw something or is he having some sort of breakdown?"

"I honestly do not know. I am very concerned. I cannot believe that he did not ask me about the child or mention her before today. We are— well, we were close. I thought he knew he could come to me with any questions or concern."

"Has he been inordinately busy the past few days? Have you spoken with him regularly?" Lucinda asked.

"Well, he has seemed a bit distant. I have been busy and I thought maybe he was giving the time he thought I needed," Frances speculated.

The two friends continued to talk and took tea while they awaited the arrival of Doctor Wellington and Catherine Todd, the spiritualist. They were interrupted by one of Frances' servants.

"Uh-um... Mrs. Catherine Todd, Ma'am," she announced as she moved to the side to let Catherine by.

"Ah, Catherine, thank you so much for coming so quickly." Lady Frances stood and hugged her friend.

"My pleasure, Frances. Now where is he?"

Lady Darlington sent Catherine to her room with a servant. Frances had him taken to her bed. She wanted him close where she could easily watch over him.

Soon another servant escorted Doctor Wellington into the room.

Lady Darlington walked to Doctor Wellington and took his hand.

"Oh, Aleister thank you for coming."

"Where is he?" Doctor Wellington asked.

"Follow me," Lady Frances said as she started to leave the room.

Lady Frances turned and asked Lucinda, "Aren't you coming?"

"Well, no. I will just wait here. I can be of no assistance," Lucinda said.

"No. You definitely can be of no assistance," Lady Frances replied with a smile. "But I am not leaving you alone in the house. I know how it unnerves you. Come now."

Lucinda could not complain. She was extremely relieved to be accompanying Aleister and Frances to check on Jack. They began their ascension up the stairs.

Lady Frances could tell by the looks on her friends' faces that they wondered why Jack would be upstairs instead of in the servant's quarters behind the main house. Alas, they did not ask, after all they allowed Ms. Poe to have a main room rather than staying in the servant's quarters. Maybe Lady Frances had a soft spot in her heart for Jack. Even though they both wondered only one asked the question.

"Frances, why is Jack up here?" Lucinda asked as they topped the stairs and walked across the landing.

"Well…" Lady Frances started but she just could finish the lie she had considered. "Jack is special to me. Let's just leave it at that. Shall we?"

Lucinda was surprised. She had never thought that Lady Frances Darlington would take a servant as a lover; however, Jack was quite pleasing to the eyes. His dark eyes were calm but penetrating and intense. He had the build of a Roman warrior. His chestnut colored hair reminded Lucinda of imperial silk. His skin was flawless and his lips were slightly full. Actually, many of the ladies had commented on his appearance.

"Of course," Aleister replied. "Your relationship with your servant is no one's business but yours. There will be no gossip from us and nothing further said."

"Of course, Frances. Your business is your business," Lucinda added.

"Thank you both," Frances replied as she opened the bedroom door. "This way."

Aleister followed as Lucinda waited in the hallway. Frances walked over to the bed and took Jack's hand in hers and sat on the edge of the bed.

She looked at Catherine Todd. "Catherine, are you all finished in here? Doctor Wellington is here to conduct his examination."

"Yes, Frances. I have completed my ritual. I will return home and mediate. I will let you know my conclusion in a day or so."

Frances let go of Jack's hands long enough to hug Catherine. She then thanked her for coming. The servant led Catherine to the door and saw her out. Frances turned back to Jack and took his hands in hers once again.

"Jack, Doctor Wellington is here. Please tell him everything so we can make certain that you are physically alright. I will leave you two now," Lady Frances said as she stood and walked back to Lucinda.

The two women sat on a small blue velvet feather filled love seat in the hallway. Lucinda took Frances' hand in hers and reassured her that Jack would be fine. That he was in the best of medical hands.

"I know Lucinda. I just really care about him," Frances confessed.

"I can see that. But what of Dorian Archer? I thought you were interested in him."

"Oh I am. I do not love Jack like that. He is there for me when I need him. I do care about him deeply. But you and I know that I could never have that kind of relationship with him. I am thoroughly taken with Dorian Archer. I could so fall in love with him— actually, I think I already have. I am just so uncertain of his feelings for me."

"If you love Jack and you want that type of relationship with him, it is possible. You know it can. Just look at Aleister and myself."

"It is different with a man of such status taking a servant girl as his wife. You know that. Men can do whatever they please and it may be frowned upon but still acceptable. Women, no matter their status or wealth, would be shunned for doing something socially unacceptable," Frances declared.

Lucinda knew that the words Frances spoke were accurate. She did not want to hurt her friend so she changed the subject to the house.

"So, tell me Frances, do you think Jack is ill or he is being haunted by the spirit of this young girl."

"I think he is being haunted but I wanted to have Aleister examine him and rule out any illness that may cause a mental break down or hallucinations."

Aleister came out after he had finished with Jack.

"Frances, he appears to be just fine to me physically. There is no fever. He doesn't appear to be ill in any manner of speaking. I am not sure why he is having visual and auditory hallucinations. I just do not know what to tell you. I have given him something to help him sleep. Just make certain he has plenty of rest for the next few days."

Frances nodded her head in acknowledgement and thanked Aleister. Lucinda wanted to lighten the mood a bit; she could tell her friend was very distraught.

"Aleister, I would like to have a dinner party and invite the Andersons, Frances and Dorian Archer. Would that be agreeable to you?"

"Of course. That sounds like a splendid idea."

"Wonderful. I had already told Frances that you would not mind at all. So we kind of had already made plans." She smiled at her husband and took his hand.

"It is good that you know me so well." He smiled at

Lucinda and kissed her on the forehead.

"Frances, if you do not mind I would like to take my wife on home now. I cancelled my appointments before I came here so I am free the remainder of the afternoon."

Frances smiled and nodded. She thanked them both and bid the couple farewell. Lucinda and Aleister took one carriage back home together and the other followed.

*****

Lucian Anderson and his wife were trying to live life as normal as possible with the most recent murders looming over everyone. They sat at the dinner table when a knock came at their door. Their servant Marie answered the door and shortly after entered the dining hall.

"I am sorry to disturb you, but this message just arrived. It is from Doctor and Mrs. Wellington. I thought it might be important." Marie curtseyed and then handed the note to Lucian.

Victoria looked on in curiosity. "What is it, Lucian? Is something the matter?"

Lucian smiled. "No my dear. It is a dinner invitation."

Victoria smiled back at her husband. "When?"

"This Saturday night at seven."

"What is the occasion?"

"It does not say. Only that they request our company."

"Will we be able to attend?" Victoria asked.

"Why, of course. What reason should we have to decline?"

"Your work. I wasn't certain... you know if something were to happen. If you were needed? If you were called out."

"I will decline. Let's just hope I am not needed," he tried to comfort his wife.

"This will be nice."

Chapter 12

Dorian Archer was sitting at his desk looking over a dinner invitation from the Wellingtons when Chief Inspector Anderson walked up to Archer's desk. Archer was perplexed by the invite he didn't even notice the Chief Inspector's presence. He and the Wellingtons had been acquaintances for years and he had been invited to many events at the Wellington's home but never something as intimate as a dinner.

"Inspector? Archer, are you alright?" the Chief Inspector asked.

"Um— yes. I'm so sorry, Chief Inspector I didn't see you there. My mind is elsewhere," Inspector Archer apologized.

"What has your attention so completely?"

"It's nothing— just a dinner invitation to the Wellingtons tomorrow night."

"Splendid. I hope are going to accept. Victoria and I will be there as well as Lady Darlington, I believe."

At the mention of Lady Frances Darlington's name Dorian Archer's ears perked up like a cat hunting a mouse. "Lady Darlington will be there? Why this strange mixture of company? I did not consider myself close enough to the Wellingtons to be invited to an intimate dinner with their closest friends."

"Well to be honest, my Victoria confided in me.

She says that Lady Darlington is quite taken with you, but you have not called upon her and was most curious to see what your feelings were for her. Lucinda Wellington is taken with romance and matchmaking so she is having this dinner so that you and Lady Darlington will have time together. Please do not repeat this. Victoria should have my head if she found out, then you would have another murder on your hands." The Chief Inspector smiled.

Dorian was even more perplexed finding this out. Why would lady Darlington be interested in him? He was just an inspector, she was a Lady and with great means. "Is Lady Darlington seeing anyone? I thought she had many gentleman friends knocking at her door. Why is she interested in my feelings?"

"Lady Darlington is not as conservative as the rest of London. She is always being pursued by eligible bachelors. However none have stolen her heart. You should go," the Chief Inspector said and he pecked on the top of Inspector Archer's desk.

"I shall," Inspector Archer said with determination.

Just as that conversation ended, a new one was brought forth by another officer who approached the two men.

"Chief Inspector Anderson, Inspector Archer there has been another murder. This one is at the stables and it is no less grim as the others. You are needed on the scene."

"Very well. We will be on our way," Chief Inspector Anderson replied as he sighed.

The two men gave one another a solemn and tiresome look. The murders kept racking up as the list of suspects were almost nonexistent. It appeared as though this murderer would not be slowing down anytime soon.

Chief Inspector Anderson and Inspector Archer grabbed their coats and hats and briskly walked to the most recent crime scene. Neither spoke until they reached their destination.

"Chief Inspector," Miller, one of the officers on duty greeted Chief Inspector Anderson.

"Miller, do we know the victim?"

"Yes, Sir. She is a lady of the night. She lived just over there," Officer Miller pointed across the street from the stables to a small shabby building. "She lived in one of the ground flats with two other woman of the same profession."

"Have you located her flat-mates yet?" Inspector Archer asked.

"No, Sir. We have tried but with no luck."

The two men walked over and even though they should have been accustomed to these scenes by then, they still gasped at the sight their eyes beheld; a woman partially clothed, throat cut from ear to ear— cut so deep that the head was almost severed from the body. Her torso was cut from neck to navel and her heart had been removed, however it was not at the scene— it had been taken. Other organs lay strewn about the body and the stable.

Chief Inspector Anderson conducted his part of the investigation and left Inspector Archer and the others to finish. He went back to his office to wait on their report. While he waited, he looked through the evidence from the other murders. They were so eerily similar to the original Ripper murders. His heart shuddered as he briefly considered Victoria. He shook the thought off almost as quickly as it had entered his mind. He thought she was with him asleep— wasn't she?

He held his head in his hands, silently contemplating anyone who could be responsible. A knock came at his door and the voice of Dorian Archer said, "Chief Inspector, we have finished. What now?"

"Now we go and speak to the only real suspect, or witness, we have at this point."

"Judge Smith?"

"Yes, as badly as I hate to, we must speak to him and see if he has an alibi for last night."

Chief Inspector Anderson stood and walked to the door, retrieved his hat and coat, and the two men took a carriage to Broderick Smith's home.

*****

It had been nearly a week since the three murders at the pub and Lilly was still staying with Broderick. Broderick had not been back to work since. They had found a new place in their relationship. Broderick realized what a wonderful woman he was about to marry and Lilly realized how much they really loved each other and just how fragile Broderick could be.

They had cried together, laughed together, and spent many hours planning their future together. The two young lovers were in the parlor of Lilly's home when a knock came at her door. In a matter of minutes, Broderick's servant girl announced Chief Inspector Lucian Anderson and Inspector Dorian Archer.

Broderick stood and greeted his unexpected guests with a handshake. "Chief Inspector Anderson, Inspector Archer, have you any updates?"

"Not on those murders. However, we discovered another victim. This one was at the stables," Inspector Archer announced.

"Oh my God. That is terrible. Were there any witnesses? Do you know who the woman was?"

"There were no witnesses. But we do know that she was a prostitute and her name was Violet Marsh. She lived just across the street from the stables. She had two flat-mates but we cannot locate them. We fear that they may have met with a terrible end as well," Inspector Archer replied.

"So, can you tell us where you were last night Broderick?" Chief Inspector Anderson asked grimly.

"I was here with Lilly. We have barely left the house since— well you know. Am I a suspect in this one as well?"

"We just want to rule you out. And you have never been formally classified as a suspect in the other three. We are still treating you as a witness in those. Please do you have a few minutes to speak with us?"

"Of course," Broderick said as he sat and gestured to his guests to sit as well. Lilly had remained seated and Broderick was now seated once again beside her.

Inspector Archer began by asking if Lilly wanted to leave the room during the gory details of the murder. She declined. He continued with the details as Broderick visibly became more shaken with every word. However, Lilly did not waver, she was almost unresponsive, almost cold.

"The stable manager came in this morning and found her. I have officers asking the neighbors and local store owners if they can give any information, but so far there is nothing more than she was found dead and mutilated and her flat-mates have still not been located," Chief Inspector Anderson concluded.

"So, can you tell us where you were last evening from dusk until dawn?" Inspector Archer asked.

"Um— yes, of course. I was here with Lilly all night. We had a late meal, played cards, talked and then retired to bed around midnight, I think," Broderick responded.

"Ms. Meriwether can you confirm Judge Smith's whereabouts?" Inspector Archer asked.

"Of course. He was here with me all night," she snapped becoming agitated with their suspicions.

"Ms. Meriwether, I understand your frustration, but can you not understand ours?" Chief Inspector Anderson asked.

"No. Frankly, I cannot. What does it matter? These are merely whores, a menace on society. Maybe this ripper is doing us all a favor cleaning the streets. I know he has done me a tremendous favor. My fiancé is now a changed man. He will never again seek the company of a whore rather than coming home to my loving arms. So I ask again gentleman: What does it really matter?" Lilly blurted out.

Broderick tried to calm her down but she jerked away from him and stormed from the room.

"Excuse me, gentlemen. I apologize for Lilly's behavior. She has been under a bit of a strain. You can understand."

"Actually, I understand the strain, we are also under an immense strain as well, however we do not condone the murders of these women," Inspector Archer replied.

"We apologize for the interruption. We will go now and we did not intend to cause Lilly to be so upset. We will keep in touch. Thank you," Chief Inspector Anderson said.

The two men rose and let themselves out while Broderick sat and thought about what his precious sweet Lilly said. He wondered if she were capable of ridding the streets of London of this vermin as she had called the prostitutes many times when speaking to Broderick. He slumped over and held his head in his hands in worry.

Lilly heard the men leave and she returned to the parlor. She stood and stared at him sympathetically until he realized he was being watched and looked up.

"Lilly, are you alright?"

"I am. I should apologize for my outburst. It was very unladylike and frankly inhuman. I should not have said what I did about those women. I just feel so frightened for you. I blame them. If you had not been lured in by them you would not be in this situation."

Broderick was taken aback by the revelation of his fiancé's feelings and her openness about sharing them. He did not want to get into a debate with her about the evil of taking a life, even of those whom some would perceive as subhuman. He simply accepted her apology and said he understood her emotions.

They went to bed early that evening. They had been sharing a bed but not in a sexual manner, Lilly was very virtuous and would not give herself to him until their wedding night. But merely having her in his arms was enough for him. He needed her love and her company—especially now.

He fell asleep holding her in his arms. Little did he know that she was still awake. Lilly did not sleep as well as Broderick did.

Chapter 13

That evening Dorian Archer stayed late and went through new Ripper files and old Ripper files. It was becoming increasingly hard to keep these murders from being named Ripper murders in the public. He was determined to solve this; there had been too many murders already and he was not thrilled about the thought of more.

The silence of the room was deafening. It was so loud that Dorian Archer awoke from the deafening stillness of the night. Everyone else in the station had long since left. Dorian had studied over the files until he had fallen asleep. As he looked out the window at the darkened streets, he wondered if there would be another victim in the morning. They had still not located Violet's flat-mates. He sat a long moment before finally urging enough courage forward to get up and go home.

He left his desk as it was and hoped that no one would disturb it when they came in. He knew he would probably be late getting back in the morning. He grabbed his coat and hat and began walking to his home. Archer's thoughts ran deep as the images of the dead flooded his mind. He was lost in his thoughts when he came upon something— something he could not believe.

He heard a woman scream and that's when he saw it.

"Hey you! Halt! I command you to turn and halt. I am Inspector Dorian Archer."

The hooded figure fled quickly into the night.

Dorian could not believe how quickly the cloaked figure had disappeared from view. And he could not believe what the figure had been slumped over and what he had been doing.

Dorian Archer ran to where the figure had been and found a woman lying on the ground. Her throat had a small incision. The Ripper had begun but had not been able to finish what he had started. Inspector Archer pulled out his handkerchief and gave it to the woman to hold on her wound.

"You stay here. I will be back," Inspector Archer instructed the woman.

She did as she was told and he bound out after where he had seen the cloaked figure disappear in the shadows. He knew his attempt at capturing the suspect was futile, but he had to at least try. Inspector Archer looked all about him and found no sign of the person in the black cloak— nothing that is except for a few grapes lying on the ground at Inspector Archer's feet.

The inspector made his way back to the woman. She was shaken but none the worse for wear. She was sobbing uncontrollably. He helped her to her feet and took her to the hospital.

There were no doctors there but there were several nurses. Upon entering he called out to a nurse, "Can you help us please? This woman was attacked and has been injured."

The nurse rushed over and took the woman to an exam room. Inspector Archer followed. He asked the woman questions as the nurse tended her wounds.

"What is your name?"

"Debra Morrison, sir. Thank you so much for saving me. I just knew I was done for. I knew that the Ripper had made his claim on me and I was surely to be next on his list."

The nurse looked at the woman and then at Inspector Archer. "The Ripper? Have these been officially ruled as Ripper murders?" she asked Inspector Archer.

"No, Ma'am, by no means have these been classified as Ripper murders. No one claiming to be Jack the Ripper has claimed responsibility. We are not sure who is doing this," he plainly stated.

He then turned his attention back to Debra. "Debra, can you give me a description of the attacker?"

"I'm sorry, I can't. They wore a mask, so I cannot even tell you if it was a woman or a man. I can't tell you the color of their hair or anything," she sobbed.

He continued his questioning but got nothing of use from her. After the nurse assigned Debra to a bed he instructed her not to leave until he and Chief Inspector Anderson came back the next morning. He left her and went back to the station to work until the Chief Inspector came in.

The Chief Inspector was the first to arrive. He found Dorian Archer with his head down on his desk and in the same clothes as the day before.

"Dorian? Have you been here all night?"

Dorian roused and sat up slowly. "What time is it?"

"It is 8 AM. Have you been here all night?"

"Not exactly. I left but I wasn't gone long and I

came back to wait on you."

"Why? Is something wrong?"

Dorian Archer explained to Chief Inspector Anderson everything that had happened the night before. The Chief Inspector could not believe his ears. They almost had this copycat Ripper. Dorian Archer had him within his grasp and he slipped threw his fingers. At least Dorian was able to save the woman.

They went to the hospital to speak with Debra further. She could tell them no more than she had told Inspector Archer the night before.

Chief Inspector Anderson told Inspector Archer to go home and rest, to take the day off. "Dorian, get some rest. I will see you tomorrow night at the Wellington's, won't I?"

"Thank you. I am exhausted. I do need the rest. Yes, I do believe I will take the Wellingtons up on their invitation. It would do me well to have a distraction. I will see you tomorrow night. If anything arises today would you please send a messenger?"

"Of course. Now go and rest."

"Thank you, Chief Inspector."

Chief Inspector Anderson went to the station and Inspector Archer went to his home to rest. It felt as if he had been working for weeks, even though he had only a couple of days of much work and little sleep. He found his way to his home and to his bed where he collapsed and slept all day and most of the night. He awoke just before dawn and felt unbelievably rested. He made himself some coffee and drank as he prepared his breakfast.

He sat and had his breakfast alone as he had done for all of his adult years. He was tired of this solitude life. Maybe his friend was right, maybe Lady Darlington was taken with him. Dorian had found something to be pleased about, something to look forward to in this dismal world.

Most of his life had been spent in the darkness of shadows— the darkness of the orphanage, the darkness of his job and the darkness of his solitude life. The darkness of his job had really begun to take its toll since the first of this resent rash of murders. Finally, a tiny ray of light penetrated the shadows letting him see the life that was possible for him— a life he had not before considered.

He thought of nothing but Lady Darlington— even the gruesome murders were temporarily wiped from his mind, from his thoughts. He went on about his day doing something that he had not done in years. He pulled a book from his bookshelf and read. He read from Shakespeare, he read from Romeo and Juliet. He had always longed for a love worth dying for, but wondered if it was really possible. Dorian prepared lunch and again ate alone gazing out his window pondering over a life with Lady Darlington. Could it be possible? He would find out.

Soon it was time to ready himself for dinner at the Wellingtons. He took a bath, shaved, put on his best suit, and combed his hair carefully. He took a coach to the Wellingtons. He sat in the coach for a few moments; having arrived a bit early he did not want to appear anxious. After a few tries, the coachman coaxed him out so that he could take care of his other fares.

Reluctantly, but anxiously, Dorian Archer climbed down from the coach and straightened his clothing and hair methodically. He took a deep breath and slowly walked to the door. Reaching up, he took the wrought iron ring on the doorknocker and smacked it hard three times against its base making for a loud bang, bang, bang. Ms. Poe was quick to answer the door— she arrived almost immediately after the third knock.

"Hello, Inspector Archer, please come in," Ms. Poe said as she took his coat and hat and hung them up. "Follow me. You are the first to arrive. I will let the Wellingtons know you are here."

Ms. Poe led him into the parlor and gestured for him to sit. "Please make yourself comfortable. They will be in soon."

"Thank you very much," Dorian said as he sat in a nearby chair. He looked around, thinking what a meager place his home was. He was always amazed at the houses the people of this stature lived in. He often wondered why there was a need for so many rooms— so much space. He was quite content in his home, but he wondered what it would be like to have so much. These thoughts brought him back to Lady Darlington and why she was interested in him.

He heard a knock at the door and the voices of two women; one was Ms. Poe and the other was the unmistakable sweet voice of Lady Frances Darlington. He was very surprised at the butterflies in his stomach and the increasing amount of moisture accumulating in his palms. He moved around in his seat sitting up straighter, ran his fingers through his hair making sure that no hair was stray, straightened his tie and smoothed out the wrinkles in his clothing.

His trouble did not go unnoticed. Lady Darlington was surprised that he was already there; she thought she was the first. She always came early as she liked being the first to arrive at any event. As soon as she saw him her heart sped up and an involuntary smile spread across her face, revealing her beaming pearly whites. She absently mindedly pushed an unruly strand of hair behind her ear and smoothed out her dress from bodice to tail. And Lady Frances Darlington did something she knew she had never done before— she blushed.

Dorian Anderson stood and walked to her. He bowed in respect and looked up at her with the biggest smile that had ever graced his lips. He reached down and took her hand; he brought it up to his mouth and lightly brushed her silky flesh with his lips.

"Lady Darlington. What a pleasure."

"Oh, Inspector, you are too kind."

"Please, don't address me as Inspector. I should prefer not to have business be a part of this evening. Please call me Dorian," he said.

"Then you should call me Frances. Let's just leave the formalities outside tonight."

"Very well, Frances."

"Thank you very much, Dorian."

Lucinda and Aleister walked in on the tail end of this conversation. Aleister smiled and added, "Then by all means, please address us as Aleister and Lucinda." He walked over and shook Dorian's hand as Lucinda and Frances hugged one another. Then Aleister kissed Frances' hand and Dorian politely kissed Lucinda's hand.

"I was surprised to receive your invitation. However, I would like to thank you so much for the invitation. I really need the distraction after the cases I have been investigating, especially the one from night before last," Dorian said.

Aleister replied, "Ah, yes, the young lady named Debra Morrison— I checked in and released her yesterday afternoon. Physically, she was well so unfortunately she will undoubtedly be back on the streets within a day or two."

"Yes, and the next time the odds will not be in her favor. But there is nothing we can do," Dorian added.

There was a final knock at the front door. It was the Andersons. Ms. Poe graciously greeted them and led them into the parlor to join the others.

"Chief Inspector and Mrs. Anderson," Ms. Poe announced.

"Ah, Lucian. Victoria. It is so good to see you." Aleister greeted Lucian with a handshake and Victoria with a kiss on the hand, Lucian greeted Lucinda with a kiss to the hand and the ladies hugged. The Andersons also greeted Dorian and Frances in the same manner.

"Please, sit everyone. Dinner shall be served soon. I would like to thank you for coming. I thought this would be a nice get together. We haven't really had the opportunity to spend much time together lately," Aleister directed toward Lucian, Victoria and Frances. Then he said to Dorian, "And Dorian, we haven't had the opportunity to get to know one another very well. Lucian speaks highly of you and I know that you two are close. I thought it would be nice to get better acquainted. I am very happy that you accepted our invitation."

"I would like to get to know you all better. It would

be nice to have people to consider friends. I have spent too much of my life devoted to my profession. It saddens me for it to have taken these murders to discover the need for companionship." Dorian smiled.

Frances slid her hand around Dorian's arm and smiled seductively up at him. "I am looking forward to getting to know you better."

Dorian was taken by surprise by Frances' boldness, nevertheless pleased. "As am I." Dorian smiled back.

Ms. Poe came in and announced that dinner was served.

"Shall we then?" Aleister said as he gestured toward the door allowing his guest to exit first.

They waited in the hall and Aleister led the way to the dining hall. The men pulled the seats out for the women and then they sat. Almost immediately, Ms. Poe led several servants in bringing mouthwatering food. Everyone was served and the servants left.

Aleister held up his glass. "I would like to make a toast. Even though the times are dark, friendship brings light. To you— my friends."

They all held up their wine-filled glasses and said in unison, "Cheers,"

Dorian Archer had a feeling warm his heart like never before. He had always considered Lucian Anderson a friend and a mentor, but he had no idea that Lucian thought so highly of him. And now to have been invited into this exclusive circle of friends was surreal. He felt included and a part of something. Even though he had been at the police station for years, he never felt like he was really a part of anything. He always felt disconnected someway. The only connection he felt there was the connection with Lucian.

Frances noticed Dorian smiling and wondered what he was thinking. They exchanged pleasantries throughout the meal. Servants came and went. In time the dinner conversation turned macabre, centering around the murders. It made Aleister, Lucinda, Lucian and Victoria a bit uneasy, but when its concentration was on the present murders they relaxed and were able to join in more freely.

"So, tell us about this young lady you saved from the murderer. Enlighten us on the events," Lady Darlington prompted.

Dorian flushed slightly not wanting to be in the spotlight, not considering himself a hero by any means— just a man whose dumb luck happened to help save a young woman from a murderer. He told his story modestly.

"Come now, Dorian, I think you are being way too modest. Your actions saved a woman," Frances continued with her flirting and flattery.

"My actions were as any other gentleman's would have been in the same situation," he said.

After a time, Lucinda stepped in to save Dorian. "Frances, I believe you are embarrassing Dorian. Let's move this topic and conversation into another room. Shall we?"

"Splendid idea," Aleister agreed.

The men pulled the chairs out for the women and they took their leave back to the parlor where they had coffee. They enjoyed pleasant conversation, coffee, and pastries. They played charades and, for a short time, there were no thoughts of murder, nor of the macabre world that lay just outside their doors.

An enjoyable and enchanting evening finally came to an end. Aleister and Lucinda saw their guests out and bid them good night and farewell.

Victoria and Lucian went home to their precious son. Dorian offered to share a carriage with Frances and to see her home safely. She graciously accepted. The first mile or two was in virtual silence with the exception of the trotting of the horse hooves beating the ground in a rhythmic *clipity-clop*. The carriage swayed and rocked the couple back and forth.

Frances spoke after much contemplation of what to say, "I enjoyed your company this evening. I am very happy that you accepted the invitation. I must confess to you though, this little soiree was for my benefit. You see, Lucinda, Victoria and I have been friends for almost ten years. We met at Lady Kinsington's while attending school together. We became very close during the first rash of Ripper murders. We stayed close until about the last year and a half. I continued my escapades and they both became pregnant. Don't get me wrong. I am very happy for them both. I just feel that my life choices have taken me down a very lonely road. Just when I thought my destiny was to always be alone, you graced my door step. I felt an instant connection— an instant spark. I thought you did too, especially when you agreed to escort me to the Wellington's Ball, but then I did not hear from you afterwards. Lucinda thought it would be a great idea to have this dinner and bring us together again. I really need to know if you are interested in me at all. If not, I understand and I will leave you be."

"My. That was a long explanation of a confession. I

hear confessions everyday, but none like that." He smiled at her.

"I am very flattered and very interested in you. And like you, I have made life choices that kept me solitary. I buried myself in my job to keep me distracted from life. Now I will give you a confession." He smiled and continued, "You see, not many know that I was an orphan and many times I was left to the streets alone to fend for myself. Shortly after I turned seventeen Lucian found me on the streets and helped me. He gave me a room in his home and helped me to get a job at the station as a messenger and an errand boy. I worked my up in the ranks fast. I moved out on my own and just kept my nose to the grindstone. I never gave a woman or really anyone but Lucian the chance to get close to me. I had been abandoned and hurt so many times that I chose to be alone rather than to be hurt by anyone. But I think fate has brought us together. I do not like the circumstance under which it happened, but nevertheless we have met. I do feel that we have a connection and I would like to pursue you if you will give me permission."

"Oh my. I was unaware of you childhood. I am very sorry to hear that it was so unkind. I, too, was orphaned but was lucky in that I was already seventeen and my parents left me servants, wealth and a high societal status. So it was not physically hard on me, but I do miss my parents very much. There is not a day that goes by that thoughts of them do not grace my mind." Frances paused momentarily and then continued, "I am very pleased to give you permission to pursue me." She smiled and the moonlight reflected from her beautiful white teeth.

The carriage ride was over far too quickly for either of their liking.

"Well, it appears that we have arrived at your mansion, Frances."

"It does in deed. Mr. Dorian Archer, I am sure that you know I do not hold to traditional considerations of what a lady should and should not do. So I am going to do something very unacceptable. I am going to invite you in for a brandy."

"If you are sure, I would love to. I did not relish the idea of us parting so soon after admissions of our feelings for one another. I will accept your invitation."

"Very good," she smiled at Dorian and then turned to the coachman. "Kind sir, you can leave. I will take care of Inspector Archer from this point forward."

The coachman gave a disapproving look to Frances and said, "As you wish, Madam." He slapped the reigns on the horses backs and left.

"How will I return home? I do not want to disturb your coachman this late."

"You can stay in a guest room and return in the morning. This will give us all night to get to know one another." Frances smiled seductively and led him into her home.

Dorian had a slight panicked feeling like a fly being drawn into a spider's web but the feeling was fleeting. He followed her into her parlor where she did something else very unladylike. She removed her shoes and unbuttoned the top two buttons of her dress.

She noticed his unease and giggled. "Don't worry, Dorian. I will not bite nor will I throw myself at you. I simply cannot stand being uncomfortable in my own home.

Feel free to make yourself more comfortable."

They had drinks and talked. They laughed and shared secrets. After many hours, they noticed a chime from the pendulum in the hallway as it chimed six times. They suddenly realized the sun was rising.

"Well, Mr. Archer, it appears you have survived a night alone with me," Frances smiled.

Dorian suddenly felt bold and an urge took him over completely— an urge to take Frances in his arms and kiss her. And he did.

Frances was taken by surprise but was pleased. His arms felt strong around her— safe. The warmth of his mouth enveloped her senses. His heavy breathing aroused her immensely. She took his face in her hands and enjoyed the slight roughness of his five o'clock shadow that had developed overnight. Then she ran her fingers through the silkiness of his hair.

Her touch brought sensations to Dorian that he had never before encountered. He felt alive and good. He felt exhilarated. He felt the sensation that he had avoided too long— a longing to be with someone.

Their kiss was long, passionate and breathless.

Dorian pulled pack and looked deeply into Frances' eyes. "I am so sorry. I just— I couldn't help myself. The urge was just so overwhelming— irresistible even." He reached up and touched her face.

Frances smiled and admitted, "If you had not kissed me, I had every intention of kissing you before this night was over."

They embraced intimately, unaware that they head been watched most of the night. Jack had kept a watchful eye on his Lady to ensure her safety. When Dorian left, Jack went back to his room.

Frances made her way to her bedroom where she undressed and readied herself for bed. It was Sunday after all, and she had never been one to attend Sunday services so she would sleep until lunch. She had no sooner crawled into bed than she heard a faint knock at her door accompanied by a whisper.

"Lady. May I enter?" Jack's comforting bass voice called out.

Frances jumped from her bed and bound to the door, opening it quickly.

"Jack, what are you doing up? You should be in bed. I told you to rest. You can begin working again first thing Monday morning."

"I just wanted to tell you goodnight. I did not get to speak to you when you came home last night. I noticed your company left," Jack admitted sadly.

"Jack. That is so sweet. Were you up all night?"

"Yes, Ma'am. I wanted to make certain you were safe."

Frances felt saddened. The relationship she had with Jack may be coming to a halt and she had not realized in all this time that he loved her. She felt so guilty and she had no idea what to do. The last thing she wanted to do was hurt him. He had been such a comfort to her.

"Thank you, Jack. That was kind. You go on to bed

now. I will see you as soon as I wake."

"As you wish."

Her heart sank when he walked away. She knew she was the reason behind his sadness. She went on in her room, got back into bed, and slid under the covers. She should have felt elated, but instead she felt conflicted. Her slumber was restless and when she arose, she felt more tired than she had when she lay down.

She called for her maids to help her bathe. The warm water and rose oil brought her back to life. She felt refreshed. After bathing and dressing, Frances went down to eat. To her surprise, Jack was already downstairs in the kitchen. He was keeping the fire to cook her food.

"Jack, why are you up? You should still be resting,"

"I could not rest. So I thought I would help with the fire."

"Bring two plates to the dinning hall please," she instructed the maid assisting the cook.

She took Jack by the hand and led him into the dining hall to dine with her.

"Please sit. I would like to talk with you while we eat."

"I can't eat in here. I am your servant," Jack protested.

"I don't consider you my servant; I consider you an employee and more than that— my friend. A dear friend. Please sit with me."

Jack pulled Frances' chair out and pushed her up to

the table. He then sat beside her.

The maid served them. At first, the meal was unnaturally quiet. Frances did not know how to start this conversation or even what she wanted to say. Finally, she broke the silence.

"Jack, we need to talk about last night."

"There is nothing to say. You are the lady of the house. I wanted to make certain of your safety. You are obviously interested in the Inspector. He is apparently interested in you. One would have to be blind not to be interested in you."

His words were breaking her heart. She had no idea that he cared so deeply for her. Her beautiful eyes watered until she could hold back no more. Tears trickled down her face.

Jack jumped to his feet and went to her side. He held her hand as he knelt by her. He reached up with one hand and wiped away her tears.

"Why are you crying?" Jack asked.

"I feel so badly. I feel that I have led you to think that our relationship was one of lasting life. I do care for you— enough that your pain saddens me deeply, especially because I am the reason you hurt."

"It is alright. I knew that we could never be married. I just thought that we would always be, well you know. I was just surprised to see you with him. I had no idea."

"I went to a dinner party that he was attending. We enjoyed one another's company and he wanted to see me home. I do really like him. I just don't know what I am supposed to do. You and I can never marry. He and I could. I never thought I would find a man that I could love."

"Really. I know my place. I will be here for you if he hurts you or if you need me for anything. I would do anything for you." He kissed her hand and said, "You needn't say another word." He stood and left the room.

Still crying she stared at his half eaten dish, feeling guilty she couldn't finish her meal.

Chapter 14

It was a new day and Broderick felt that it was time to go back to work. Now that there had been another murder and he had an alibi, maybe he would no longer be a under suspicion. And news had found its way to him there had been an attempted murder a few nights prior; yet no one had come to question him.

Lilly had continued her watchful eye over her beloved Broderick. She had so enjoyed having him all to herself for so many days and nights. Their wedding day could not come soon enough.

"Broderick, must you go to work today. It such a dreadful and dreary place— that courtroom with all of those criminals whose fate you should decide. It seems like too much responsibility."

"Lilly, my dear. Your father is too a judge. Do you feel this way about his working in the courts?"

"I just feel it's a waste of time. You convict these criminals, they serve their time, and then are released to commit yet another crime. It is a never-ending cycle. Do you suppose—"

"Do I suppose what?" Broderick asked.

"Do you suppose that the murderer could be someone from the court, possibly a judge? You know Judge Whitman went missing about ten years ago, right around the time that the Ripper murders ended. My father said that he was a suspect."

"I do not know. That is something I had not considered. I just hope that I am dropped from suspicion."

"Don't worry, my love, if they persist I will make sure my father puts an end to this ridiculous inquisition," she put her hands up and held his face.

She stepped up on her tiptoes and kissed him on the mouth. He returned the kiss with passion and fervor. He thought to himself why had he had so many relations with other women? Why had he betrayed her so?

"I don't think involving your father will be necessary. But thank you for trying to protect me. I know now the love that you hold for me. You have shown the love that I do not deserve. I hope that I can show you the love that I hold for you for the rest of my life. I swear to you, that I will never betray your love or trust again."

He embraced her closely and tightly for the longest minute, then pulled back and kissed her on the forehead. "I really must leave now. Will you be here when I return tonight or will you return to your father's house?"

"I will be here. I plan on going to visit my mother and I will be back here before you return."

"Does you father not object to you staying here with me?"

"I am a woman. He has no jurisdiction over me. I come and go as I please."

"Very well. I will see you when I return. I do adore you. I do love you."

Broderick kissed her once more, this time on the cheek. He left to spend the day in the courts.

*****

Lucian awoke to his wonderful wife, who lay beside him still sleeping soundly. He stroked her face and admired her strength. He kissed her lightly on the cheek, however, not lightly enough.

Victoria awoke with a smile on her face and warmth in her heart.

"Lucian. This weekend was much too short. Can you not take today with me?" she pleaded and then reached up and kissed him on the mouth.

"I am so sorry, my love. I must go. We must find the one behind these murders. And we must try to keep prying eyes from looking too closely into the past murders."

"Well, I need a few things from the bakery, so can we have lunch together?"

"Of course. I would love that. What will you bring for us to eat?"

"I have not thought of that. I think it shall be a surprise to you— and to me." She smiled.

"Very well then surprise me."

Lucian kissed Victoria deeply and leaned back with a sigh.

"Oh, my sweet Victoria, I must get up and get to work."

"I know," she said as she watched him get up and get changed. She loved to watch him in anything that he did. She loved to watch him take a cigar and brandy after a long hard day. She loved to watch him read. She especially loved to watch him spending time with his son being the perfect father.

"Alright, if you must leave me then I shall get up and start my day as well."

Victoria finally pulled herself from her feather-filled pillow and her warm blankets. She shed her nightgown, which immediately caught Lucian's eye as he pulled up his suspenders. She put on her dress and Lucian helped her with all of the ties and buttons. He pulled her closely and kissed her, then whispered in her ear, "I love you."

"I know that well. And I love you."

They went down to breakfast hand in hand. As they sat over their plates, Victoria made the decision to ask a long-awaited question.

"Lucian, are there really no suspects?"

"Not really. There was only Broderick Smith but then he had an alibi for this last murder. However, Lilly Meriwether did have a strange reaction when we went by to question him. And she said the strangest thing. She was very hostile and said that she could not understand why we were so concerned with these murders, that maybe this murderer was cleaning the streets of London."

"That was odd. I have known Lilly for several years. She is a bit snobbish, but I have never known her to be cruel."

They finished breakfast and Lucian left for work.

Victoria concluded her household obligations for

the morning and took a carriage to the bakery. She decided to purchase bread and pastries at the bakery for lunch and then pick up some fruit and cheese from the market and wine from the winery. Extremely pleased with herself, she thought this was a wonderful idea for lunch. However, before she could finish her purchases at the market she bumped into Lilly Meriwether.

"Hello, Lilly. You look absolutely lovely today."

"Thank you. As do you. What a pleasant surprise," Lilly responded.

Even though her response was pleasant, it seemed forced. Victoria could tell. She felt as though Lilly was somehow upset with her.

"Lilly, is everything alright?"

That one small question set off an unexpected outburst. Lilly's response stunned everyone in the market and left Victoria both confused and hurt.

"I would be just fine if your husband and that side kick of his would leave Broderick and myself alone."

"I must say. I don't know what you are talking about," Victoria lied, knowing that an admission of the truth could cost Lucian his job.

"You know exactly what I am talking about. I know your husband tells you things— things pertaining to his work, to these murders. You can tell him Broderick had nothing to do with any of them and if the police do not back down my father will have the jobs of every man there and replace them with men of competence— men who will stop harassing us and find the true murderer."

"I am very sorry. I really do not know anything about my husband's work cases, but rest assured I will give him your message. And good day, Lilly," Victoria said politely, even though her blood was boiling inside from the attack on her husband's character and competence.

Lilly went on her way as she stuck her nose in the air.

Victoria finished collecting the things she needed for both home and lunch with her husband. She needed to tell him what had happened with Lilly but did not know how or when. She contemplated that while she finished her shopping and finally decided just before entering the police station that she should tell him right away in the privacy of his office.

Lucian's eyes lit up when he saw his beautiful Victoria. He ushered her into his office and closed the door behind them. He quickly and swiftly brought her into his arms and kissed her.

"This is indeed a pleasantry. I am very pleased that you suggested this. It will be a nice distraction from this horrid case."

Victoria had a strange look about her and bit her lower lip. Lucian knew this to be the look of his wife needing to tell him something important— something that would be upsetting, but something that she would rather someone else tell him.

"I recognize that look and I do not particularly like it. What has happened?"

Victoria thought it best not to beat around the bush, just say it and get it over with.

"I saw Lilly Meriwether today at the market. She was extremely upset and said a few things that were very disturbing and her tone was very hurtful." Lilly continued her story and told Lucian everything that Lilly had said.

"I am very sorry that my professional position has put you at odds with one of your friends."

"Oh no, Lucian, I do not put any blame on you at all. We all know that this whole mess would not have begun without my actions ten years ago."

"Yes, but then we would not be together today and who knows what Judge Whitman could have done to a number of people you love, including your mother and Lucinda. This is not your fault. To be honest, I am now a bit suspicious of Ms. Meriwether. Maybe we should check her alibis as well."

"Lucian, please be careful. You know her father. He will do anything to protect Lilly. I do not want you in the path of one of his rampages."

"I am sworn to uphold my job without favoritism or prejudice. I am not concerned with the Meriwethers and neither should you. I have a good man at my back anyway."

Victoria knew he was talking about Dorian Archer. Dorian was a good man— an honest and fair man. She could wish for no one better than Dorian to be at her husband's helm.

"You seem to be extremely concerned with my well-being. So tell me what you have brought me to eat," Lucian smiled at Victoria and lifted the cloth from the top of her basket.

"I have brought many good things for lunch including a bottle of wine."

Lucian looked as his wife emptied the contents of the basket on his desk. They ate and enjoyed a wonderful lunch together— that is, until it was interrupted by Inspector Dorian Archer.

"Come in," the Chief Inspector said.

"I am so sorry to interrupt you meal. I know this is a rare treat, but we have news about the flat mates of Violet Marsh."

"What is it Inspector?"

"The two flat mates of Violet Marsh have been found— dead."

"Where and when?" Chief Inspector Anderson asked.

"On the outskirts of town in a wooded area. It seems he was able to take more time with these two out of possible prying eyes."

"Why do you say that?" Chief Inspector Anderson asked.

Archer looked at Victoria with concern, not wanting to give graphic details. Chief Inspector Anderson noticed and asked Victoria to give them a moment. She did so without hesitation, she knew he would tell her everything in private.

"Well?" Chief Inspector Anderson asked impatiently.

"We cannot tell which body parts belong to which

woman and some organs are so mangled we cannot tell what they were."

"Let me get Victoria cleared up. I want to see her home and then I will meet you there. Write the directions down please."

Lucian called Victoria back in and Dorian went to fulfill Lucian's request. Lucian did not say much to Victoria until they were in the carriage. There he filled her in on what little he knew.

He saw her to the door and kissed her goodbye. Victoria could not shake the feeling that something was amiss with Lilly. And now these two gruesome murders and dismemberment. Victoria could withstand a great deal and that is why Lucian was being brutally honest with her about these murders— and the fact that they had a lot at stake if was ever discovered that Victoria was the original Jack the Ripper. If it were discovered that Judge Whitman had been murdered, he would no longer be the prime suspect in those murders.

Even though her husband had seen her safely home and wanted her to stay there, Victoria had to see her dear friend Lucinda and tell her the events of the day. Maybe Lucinda could visit Lilly and see what she thought.

Victoria called for Marie and let her know that she was going back out and to let Lucian know that she had went to the Wellington's house if he arrived back home before her. She called for the carriage and set out to see Lucida.

The carriage pulled up in front of the Wellingtons. The footman helped Victoria from the carriage and she dropped the knocker on the door but once before it was answered by Ms. Poe.

"Well hello, Mrs. Anderson, what a pleasant surprise. I will call Lucinda. You take a seat in the parlor. May I take your wrap?" she said as she reached for Victoria's wrap and then led her into the parlor.

It was only a matter of minutes before Lucinda entered. In fact, Victoria had barely had time to sit and adjust her dress.

"Victoria, this is a surprise," Lucinda said as she greeted Victoria with a hug.

"I'm so sorry to drop in unannounced. I just really needed to see you. I really needed to speak with you about something— and to ask a small favor."

"Of course. You know I would do anything for you. What is it? Is something the matter?"

"Oh no. Not really. I just had the strangest encounter with Lilly Meriwether."

"What, pray tell, happened?" Lucinda asked as she took a seat beside of her friend.

Victoria proceeded to tell Lucinda about her odd encounter with Lilly. And just as Lucian had reacted, Lucinda was very surprised at Lilly's behavior.

"Since you have no direct ties with these murder cases, I was thinking that maybe Lilly would open up to you. Maybe you could see why she had behaved in the manner she did with me. Maybe she is just upset because Broderick has been questioned by Lucian. Maybe she is taking it out on me because I am Lucian's wife. Would you care to speak her?"

"Of course not. I cannot today, but I will tomorrow.

Do you know if she is back home or if she is still staying with Broderick?"

"I do believe she is still staying with Broderick," Victoria replied. "Thank you so much, Lucinda. You are a true friend."

They talked for a while longer and as the afternoon grew into evening, Victoria excused herself and returned home only moments before Lucian.

Chapter 15

Aleister arrived that evening with a grim and disturbing look upon his face.

Lucinda could tell in an instant that something terrible was troubling her husband. She had not seen him this troubled in nearly ten years.

"Aleister. What is it? You look like so upset," she took his hand in an attempt to comfort him.

"I was called upon by Lucian and Dorian to help out in their investigation. They brought some remains in for me to— to, well to put back together," he said as he ran his fingers through his hair.

"What do you mean? What remains?"

He led Lucinda into his study and closed the door for complete privacy. "I have been sworn to secrecy. They did not even want me to share this with you. But I cannot hide anything from you. This is truly disturbing, are you certain you want to know?" he cautioned.

"Aleister, after all that we have been through, you know I need to be there for you no matter how grim the news."

They sat together on the couch as Aleister began recounting the events of his dreadful day.

"The flat mates of the last murder victim were found this morning in a wooded area on the outskirts of the city. The women were dismembered so badly that they could not tell which body parts belonged to which woman. They brought the remains to me and asked me to put them back together. It has been a gruesome day, to say the least. The two women found in the room above the pub that had been with Broderick were dismembered badly but were relatively easy to distinguish what body parts belonged to each. This time it was not only body parts, but organs. It took so long to determine what they were."

"Aleister, I am so sorry. Would you like to take dinner in the atrium tonight?"

"No, Darling. I prefer not to have dinner at all tonight. I would just like to rest. It has been a tiring day. I have not performed any procedures like this in ten years. I had forgotten what a toll it takes on the mind to see humans in such manner."

He sat back in his chair and covered his face with his hands. Lucinda came over and stood by him. She put her hand on his shoulder and laid her face on the top of his head. She closed her eyes and wished that she could do something to ease his troubled mind.

"Are you sure you won't eat anything?" Lucinda asked.

"No, thank you. You go have your meal and I will sit here and rest."

"I will be back soon," Lucinda started to walk away, but then remembered she had something to tell Aleister as well. She turned and said, "Oh, I had the strangest visit from Victoria today. Apparently, she had a slightly volatile encounter with Lilly Meriwether and asked if I could visit her tomorrow and see if I could figure out why Lilly is so upset with Victoria."

"What happened between them, exactly?" Aleister asked.

"Victoria said she ran into Lilly today and greeted her. When she did Lilly was very cruel and hurtful in her words. Lilly told Victoria to let Lucian know that if the police did not stop harassing Broderick her father would have the jobs of everyone at the station."

"Are you going to visit Lilly?"

"Well, I feel that I must. Victoria is my dearest friend and you know what she has done in the past in an effort to protect me. Do you object?"

"Of course not. Just be careful what you say and be mindful of your actions. Do not give her a reason to think that you are spying and do not give her a reason to seek vengeance on you."

"I will be careful."

"Now go and have your dinner."

Lucinda went on into the kitchen to join Ms. Poe.

"Ms. Poe, do you need any help?" Lucinda asked as she patted Ms. Poe on the back.

"No, thank you, dear. I am just about ready to serve you and Doctor Wellington."

"Well, there has been a change in dinner plans. I will not be dining with Aleister tonight. He has had a long and trying day and he has no appetite for food tonight. So I was wondering if you would like to join me in the atrium?"

"I would love to. Are you sure it is alright?"

"Of course. Have the maids bring our food to us."

"Very well," Ms. Poe smiled.

Ms. Poe gave the kitchen staff instructions. She and Lucinda walked into the atrium together. They were seated and the maids brought in their meals.

"You looked concerned as well. Is something troubling you other than the troubles of Doctor Wellington?"

"Actually, Ms. Poe, there is something troubling me. I would like to speak with you in confidence. May I?" Lucinda asked.

"You may always speak to me in confidence. You are well aware of that. What is troubling you, my dear?"

Lucinda confided in Ms. Poe about all the events of both her day and Aleister's day.

"No wonder he does not have an appetite. Is there anything I can to help you with?"

"No, thank you, Ms. Poe. Just listening was a great help. I just need someone other than Aleister to talk to— especially about these issues."

They finished their meals. Ms. Poe cleaned up and prepared the house for retiring for the evening. Lucinda went back into the study with Aleister where she found him with his head on his desk fast asleep.

"Aleister," she whispered. "Come, my love, let me help you to bed."

Weary-eyed and groggy, he roused to the sound of Lucinda's whispers.

"I do need the sleep. I still have further work to finish in the morning for Lucian."

Lucinda helped her husband up the stairs and into bed. She lay beside him and slept nuzzled in his arms soundly all night.

The next morning Aleister arose remarkably rested and ready to finish his work. Lucinda was too ready to face her day. She was anxious to discover what the issue with Lilly Meriwether was and then inform her friend of her findings.

They had breakfast and then went on their separate ways to face the day that was set before each of them.

Aleister went to work where he was awaited by the remains of two corpses. He worked deliberately and hard until it was time to call in Chief Inspector Anderson and Inspector Archer.

Lucinda called for the carriage and went to visit Lilly Meriwether. She arrived at Judge Broderick Smith's house mid-morning. Her footman helped her descend her carriage and she walked over to the front door and knocked. Broderick's maid opened the door.

"Yes. May I help you?"

"Yes. I am Lucinda Wellington. Is Lilly Meriwether here?" Lucinda asked.

"Please wait here and I will announce you."

The maid returned to retrieve Lucinda. "Ms. Meriwether will see you now. Please follow me."

Lucinda followed the maid to the parlor where Lilly was already awaiting Lucinda.

"Lucinda, it is so good to see you. To what do I owe this pleasure?"

"Well to be honest, I heard about Broderick and wanted to check on you. I apologize for not coming sooner."

"Thank you for your concern, but we are both fine. Broderick is an innocent man. The only sins against him are his relations with all those whores. But that has come to an end— I'm just sorry it had to be in the manner it was. If you have come to console me or offer pity then you can leave now. If you have come as a friend to distract me from my worries then you may stay and this discussion will find an end."

Lucinda was surprised at the frankness in Lilly's words. She knew she could find nothing out for Victoria if she let herself be insulted and left. So she stayed as much for Lilly as for Victoria. After all, she and Lilly had been friends for a while now.

Lucinda put her hand on Lilly's and said, "I am your friend. I am here as your friend. I will do what ever it takes to make you feel better and forget your concerns as a friend. You tell me what you wish to talk about and at any minute you should decide to strike the previous conversation up once again I will listen and offer my thoughts— but only on your prompting."

Lilly's face softened immediately and she smiled in relief. "It is so nice to have someone to talk to about ordinary mundane things instead of having to answer questions about Broderick and these murders. My father is the worst for criticizing and chastising. He is upset with Broderick and his promiscuity and that it has landed him in the position he is in, however, he blames Broderick for nothing. In his eyes, I am the reason Broderick has to fraternize with whores, but enough of that. I would like to discuss frivolous and unimportant matters."

"Very well. What topic do you wish?" Lucinda asked.

"Well let me see. I wish to discuss gardens. Yours is the most beautiful I have ever seen. How do you get it to be so breathtaking?"

"I have a wonderful gardener and I love to spend time in the garden myself. Aleister pokes fun at me because when I am in the gardens working with the plants I do not wear shoes. I like to feel the earth under my feet."

"Oh my goodness. I do not think I will ever have gardens as splendid as yours if that is the case. I do not like getting my hands dirty and I never walk outside without my shoes," Lilly laughed.

"Well, maybe I should come and tend your grounds as well," Lucinda joked.

Lilly laughed and sighed. "This is nice. Thank you."

"What topic should you like to discuss now?" Lucinda asked.

"Actually, I would like to ask you about Ms. Poe," Lilly said.

Lucinda was surprised by this line of discussion.

"What about Ms. Poe?"

"You and Doctor Wellington seem very close to her. Everyone notices that she is more like your family than help. What is so special about her? Why would you treat you help so well? Does it not make them soft and lazy?"

Lucinda was beginning to get perturbed, but she held steady and answered Lilly's questions.

"Ms. Poe is very special to Aleister. She helped him through the death of his parents. She was very nice to me when I came to Aleister's house a mere maid. She treated me as if I were special somehow, even though her household status was higher than the one I had ran away from. She is a wonderful person— not servant, person. Ms. Poe is there for us no matter what the need whether we need someone to listen to our troubles or someone to care for us while we are sick. I was once the help and I remember how it felt to be treated less than human because of my status. I will never be charged with that accusation," Lucinda replied defensively.

"I see I hit a nerve. I apologize. You have been such an important woman in London society for so long I had all but forgotten you had once been a servant. Now who were your employers?"

Lucinda was becoming increasingly angry but held her tongue.

"I worked for Judge Whitman for many years. He was a brutal and sadistic employer. Unlike him, his wife was like a mother and Victoria like a sister— she still is. If you don't mind I would like to change the topic this time."

"Of course. I did not mean to offend. I, and most of London, just do not understand why you treat your help so kindly. I was just inquiring. We can discuss something else. Let's see now. How about weddings since I have one coming up. Do you have any helpful suggestions?"

The two women discussed weddings, flowers,

clothing and jewelry among other frivolous things. The afternoon passed rather quickly. Finally Lucinda excused herself and left. She went to Victoria's home on the way back to hers.

When Lucinda knocked on the door, she was surprised to see Victoria answer.

"Well, have you been? Come in, come in. Tell me everything," Victoria said as she pulled Lucinda into the parlor.

"Well, she did not mention seeing you at all. She pretty much refused to speak about Broderick or the murders other than stating that she was tired of all of the questions and comments people had about Broderick's involvement. She did say that her father blamed her for Broderick's infidelity and he thought Broderick could do no wrong," Lucinda said.

"That was it?"

"Well, yes— about Broderick and the murders. But she had a very strange question for me. She inquired about my relationship with Ms. Poe and wanted to know why Aleister and I treated her as if she were family. She also questioned with whom I had been employed before running away."

"Those are strange questions. Did she give any indication as to why she was inquiring?"

"No. I informed her that the conversation was making me uncomfortable and I wanted to discuss something else."

"And?" Victoria asked.

"And we discussed every frivolous thing under the sun. At first, she seemed that she needed a friend to lean on, and then it was almost as if she were trying to provoke me. Then she was just going through the motions of entertaining. It was almost as if she were relieved when I left," Lucinda said.

"That is peculiar. Lilly is behaving quite strangely. Do you think this has all taken its toll on her and she is going mad?" Victoria asked.

"I'm not certain what is going on with Lilly. Unless she contacts me, I think I will just keep my distance from her. You would probably do well to do the same."

"I decided that when I had my confrontation with her at the market. She is losing her senses. Thank you for going to see her. I am sorry she made you feel uneasy. I should not have asked you to go, but I do feel much better in knowing that it is not just me thinking something is not quite right with her," Victoria said.

"Shall we have lunch? I had the help hold it. I was hoping you would come by before I simply starved to death," Victoria laughed.

"Thank you."

They went into the dinning hall and had a nice lunch together. The two friends laughed and talked about old times, the present, and the possible future. They then parted ways with a hug and a farewell.

*****

Evening fell and Broderick came home to find Lilly throwing a tantrum on the staff— his staff. He was so surprised; he had never before seen her behave in such a manner.

He could hear the commotion from the foyer but he was unprepared for what he walked in on. Lilly had a silver candlestick drawn and ready to strike one of the maids as Broderick rounded the corner. He was just in time to save the poor woman from being struck in the head. He grabbed Lilly's hand and wrung the candlestick from it; she did not give it up easily.

"What are you doing? What is wrong with you?" Broderick yelled.

"Your staff is incompetent! They have been nothing but trouble today," Lilly snapped back.

"What in God's name could they have to done to warrant a beating with a candlestick?"

Lilly burst into tears and fell into Broderick's arms. "I am so sorry. I just lost control. The day started off badly. First off the staff let Lucinda Wellington know I was here so I could not turn her away. I know she was here to spy for Victoria Anderson." Lilly continued to explain about her confrontation with Victoria at the market the day before and Lucinda's visit. She went on to list several issues she had with the staff throughout the day from having a dirty fork served to her to dead flowers left for two days in a vase.

"Lilly. First of all, you cannot be rude or hold the investigation against Victoria or Lucian Anderson. He is only doing his job and she has no part in his job. Secondly, Lucinda may have just come by to check on you; you two have been friends for years. And lastly, I don't run my house in the manner that your parents run theirs. I am lenient with my staff. I do not worry about old flowers and the spot on the fork was an accident. This is still my house and you will not treat my staff in any manner other than courtesy."

Broderick took a break from his lecture and sighed deeply. Lilly did not respond at all. She had stopped crying; she was stunned that Broderick had scolded her over the staff. She stepped back from his arms and just glared at him.

"Honestly, Lilly, I do not understand what has gotten into you." Broderick turned and walked from the room. He called his staff into the kitchen and made certain everyone was alright. He also asked the staff for their side of the story. He had his meal alone in the kitchen while Lilly ate in alone in the dining hall. That night they slept in different rooms. Broderick had sent her to a guest room down the hall and did not speak to her again until the next morning.

*****

Lucinda once again traveled quietly by foot and for some unknown reason down the cold dark streets of Whitechapel. Only this time, she ventured off and somehow was behind her old mansion in the gardens. Fear took her over. Once again she came upon a ghastly scene.

Lucinda came upon someone knelt beside the limp body of a woman, however this was not the body of a prostitute, this was the body of a servant— a servant she recognized. This was one of Lady Frances Darlington's servants.

Lucinda had been on these nightly travels enough by now to know that she was only dreaming. She took advantage of this knowledge and mustered up the courage to stay and to try to see whom the cloaked figure was. She was hoping to gain some knowledge that would help the

Chief Inspector.

Lucinda crept closer and closer until she was close enough to hear the breathing of the cloaked figure. She positioned herself in a manner that would allow her full view of their face if they turned around— the way the moonlight shone would illuminate the face of the fiend. So she waited and watched in horror.

The sounds of the flesh being cute and the blood being spilt as the cloaked figure pulled organs out made Lucinda feel faint. She was uncertain if she could withstand it until the figure turned— if they turned. The moonlight illuminated the corpse and the increasing flow of red that covered the body and the ground. The air carried the copper scent of blood to Lucinda's nose making her nauseous.

After what seemed like an hour of waiting, the hooded figure turned toward Lucinda and reached up to wipe a speck of blood from their face. Lucinda was shocked to see that the cloaked figure appeared to be faceless. She was so upset that her dream state had let her down by obscuring the identity of the murderer. Immediately she let herself wake.

Aleister immediately awoke to the stirring of his restless wife. He knew that her thrashing and moaning meant she was having yet another nightmare.

"Lucinda. Lucinda, are you alright? What is it?" he said as held grabbed hold of her arms, pulling her close.

"I am fine. I am just so extremely frustrated and saddened," she said.

"What is it? Was it another nightmare about the murders?"

"Yes. I realized it was but a dream so I stayed and positioned myself in a manner in which I could see the face of the cloaked figure. I endured such a long wait as they cut away at the corpse. Finally when they turned they were faceless. So it was all in vain. Why has my dream deceived me by obscuring the figure's face?" she sniffled.

"Lucinda, you did your best. You did more than most could have. Do you think it was an actual murder? Where did it occur? Do you know who the victim was?" Aleister bombarded her with questions.

"I think it probably was a true murder. It was— well, it was behind the old mansion. It was one of Frances' servants."

"Oh, my God. Why would the murderer move from Whitechapel to a residence? And a prominent residence at that."

"Should we go to the mansion? Should we go to Lucian? Should we do anything tonight?"

Aleister got out of bed and dressed as he explained his actions, "I am going to go to Lucian and then we will go to the mansion together. I will be back soon."

"I must come with you," Lucinda said as she started from the bed.

Aleister protested, "You should not accompany me. You really should not be exposed to the crime in reality, if there has indeed been a crime. Please stay here. I will be back as soon as I can."

Lucinda was not taking "no" for an answer. Aleister knew better than to argue with her when she had her mind set on something she thought was important. So he protested no longer. She dressed and he went to fetch the carriage. They did not wait on the coachman. He readied the horse and carriage and, when the time came, he drove it.

Lucinda was not far behind him. As soon as she was ready, she woke Ms. Poe and informed her of the goings on and asked her to make certain Elizabeth was cared for. Ms. Poe assured Lucinda she would take very good care of Elizabeth and told her to be careful.

Lucinda met Aleister at the front of the house. He helped her into the carriage and they were on their way. When they arrived at Lucian and Victoria's, Aleister helped Lucinda from the carriage and they quickly made their way to the door and knocked. Marie answered the door. She knew how close the two couples were and that they would not be there unless it was a dire emergency so she invited them in and went directly to wake the Andersons.

Lucian and Victoria were in the foyer in a matter of minutes. Lucinda and Aleister quickly and, as completely as possible, explained Lucinda's dream.

"I will go and get dressed. I will go and check it out immediately," Lucian said.

"I will accompany you," Aleister said.

"Very well."

"I am going as well," Lucinda announced.

Victoria quickly announced that she would also be accompanying them.

"Ladies, you cannot go. You must stay here. You are both too sensitive to the murders," Lucian said.

"I need to go. I had the dream. I may be of help," Lucinda declared.

"Please Lucinda. You both really need to stay here," Lucian insisted.

"Lucinda, you wanted to come so that Lucian could check on things. Let him do his job— without the company of two women. Don't you think it would go along much quicker with two as opposed to four? And besides, how would he explain you two? I can be explained away due to my profession," Aleister pleaded with his wife.

Lucinda conceded and Victoria was quick to follow her lead.

"Very well. We will wait here, but if you are not back by daybreak expect to see us there," Lucinda warned.

"As you wish," Lucian agreed.

The two men kissed their wives goodbye and sped away in Aleister's carriage. When they arrived at the mansion everything seemed quiet and calm. Lucian knocked on the door of the mansion. No one answered at first. He knocked several more times before Jack finally answered.

"I am so sorry. Rose usually answers the door. Her quarters are just outside the kitchen. I'm not certain why she did not come right away. She must be sleeping soundly. How can I help you? I'm sure you obviously desire to speak with Lady Darlington?"

"Yes, please. Are you in position to wake her?" Lucian asked.

Jack smiled and said, "Yes. Give me a moment.

Please be seated in the parlor."

Jack turned and retrieved Lady Darlington promptly.

Frances was still wrapping her robe around her and yawning as she entered the room.

"Gentlemen, I would say what a pleasant surprise, but if you have come at this hour I am certain that nothing pleasant can come from this visit. How can I assist you this late hour?"

Lucian began, "Frances, I apologize for coming at this hour but..." he trailed off.

Aleister stepped in, "Lucinda had a dream. She has had prophetic dreams before of these murders and the murders ten years ago. Tonight she had one about this house— actually about someone in this house."

Frances interrupted, "Oh my God, are you saying something dreadful will happen?"

"No. Actually we think something dreadful has already happened," Lucian finished.

"What? Tell me what?" Frances demanded.

"Lucinda dreamed that one of your servants was murdered and mutilated here on the grounds in the back," Aleister continued.

"Who? Who was it?" Frances asked, becoming anxious.

"We are not certain. Lucinda said it was one of your servants," Lucian explained.

"Is there a way we can check to make certain everyone is accounted for and well?" Lucian asked.

"Yes, of course," Frances said and then paused as if she had an epiphany. She turned to Jack, "Why did you wake me? Where is Rose?"

"I don't know where Rose is. I heard the knocking and came to answer the door because she did not. I have not seen her since dinner last evening," Jack replied.

Frances ran to Rose's quarters first and she was not in her room. Her bed had never been slept in. They looked at one another in horror and in fear. They all ran to the back grounds together. They spread out and began to look. Lucian and Aleister parted ways and Jack accompanied Frances so she would not be alone in the dark.

Neither Aleister nor Lucian saw anything out of the ordinary. Just as they were regrouping they heard a scream. They ran to find Frances wilted in Jack's arms screaming. When they looked down to see what she was screaming about they saw the mutilated body of a woman.

Lucian asked Jack, "Is this Rose?"

"I— I believe so. It's so hard to tell," Jack replied as he held Frances tightly, keeping her from falling to the ground.

"You should take Frances to her room where she can lay down. Do you need help getting her inside?" Aleister asked.

"I do believe she should be taken in. I can get her myself, thank you," Jack replied.

Lucian looked weary and Aleister could tell that

these murders were taking their toll on him.

"What can I do, Lucian?"

"Please go and fetch Dorian, then go back to my home and let Lucinda and Victoria know what has happened."

"What should I tell Dorian?"

"Just tell him that there has been another murder at Lady Darlington's house. Do not mention to him how we came to discover the murder. Tell him that I called upon you to help examine the body and asked that you bring him with you."

"You do not want him to know I have been here?"

"No. I will inform Frances and Jack. I think Frances will be alright with that to protect Lucinda and keep her from all of this murder business," Lucian said.

Aleister did as he was asked and sped away to retrieve Dorian Archer. Lucian went inside to speak with Frances and Jack.

Lucian went into the mansion and found Jack sitting in the parlor with his head in his hands.

"Jack," Lucian called.

Jack looked up, "Yes, Sir."

"I need to speak to you and Lady Darlington about this murder and how the body was found. Can you lead me to her room?"

"Of course, Sir."

Lucian followed as Jack led the way up the stairs to

Frances' bedroom. Jack knocked softly on the door and called to her.

"My Lady. The Chief Inspector needs to speak with you. May we enter?" Jack called out.

"Yes. Please come in," Frances answered.

Jack opened the door for Lucian. Lucian entered first and Jack followed. There was one chair beside her bed that she gestured to Lucian to sit in. Jack walked over and sat in a chair across the room.

"Jack, come over here, comfort me," Frances said as she patted the bed beside her legs.

Jack walked over and sat.

"Now, Lucian, what is it?" Frances asked.

"To be honest, I need you two to not be so honest," Lucian said.

"I don't understand. What do you mean?" Frances asked.

"We would like to keep Lucinda and her dreams or visions from the speculations of others. Is it possible for you two to say that you found her and that you sent Jack to get me?" Lucian asked.

"Of course. Lucinda has been a dear friend to me for so long. I will not say anything, however I have one request," Frances said.

"I'm certain we can accommodate you. What is your request?" Lucian asked.

"After you have finished here and the police have

left and taken Rose's poor body away, I would like for Lucinda to come and speak to me. I want to know all about her visions. You know I am fascinated with spiritualism and soothsaying. I know she tries to avoid this house, but maybe she will come and speak with me under the circumstances."

"I'm sure that won't be an issue. She is your dear friend and I am certain she will want to check on you anyway. I will give her the message," Lucian said.

Lucian explained what should be said, what should be left out and what should be changed when Frances and Jack spoke to the other policeman and everyone else. As Lucian was finishing his instructions they heard a knock at the door.

"I will answer the door and then I will be back to check on you," Jack said as he stood.

Frances reached up and took Jack's hand and smiled as she simply said, "Thank you."

*****

Aleister arrived at Dorian's modest home and pounded on the door. As he waited to be greeted, he noticed the beautiful pink Hughes of the predawn light; he found it hard to imagine such beauty in the world when he had just witnessed, once again, one of the most horrifying images in the world.

Dorian Archer answered the door with furrowed brows and half growled, "Doctor Wellington, what are you doing here at this hour? What has happened? Is your family well?"

"I have been called upon by Lucian. He has asked that I fetch you on my way. Apparently, there has been a murder at Lady Frances Darlington's mansion," Aleister explained.

Dorian's furrowed brows rose and he quickly inquired as to the wellbeing of Lady Darlington, "Is she alright? Who has been murdered?"

"Oh no. Frances is fine. I believe it was one of her servants. Lucian is there awaiting our arrival. We must go quickly."

Dorian turned to get changed then paused and turned back to Aleister, "Why has the Chief Inspector called upon you?"

"My medical expertise, I assume. You all called upon me to examine and reassemble the remains of the last two victims. I am uncertain as to why he has called upon me at this hour. Maybe because Frances and Lucinda are very close he thought my presence would be a comfort to Frances."

"Well, that makes sense. I will be back shortly. Have a seat," Dorian gestured at a chair beside the front door.

Aleister sat and waited. He admired the modest home of Dorian; he sometimes wished for simplicity.

Dorian returned within minutes. He took his coat and hat from the coat tree by the door.

"Shall we?" Dorian asked as he pointed toward the front door.

"Of course," Aleister said, nodding.

When Dorian saw there was no coachman he was surprised.

"Doctor Wellington, where is your coachman?"

"I did not want to take the time to wait on mine. I wanted to get to Lucian quickly. I thought it was imperative since he had sent for me at such an hour."

"Well, I shall ride with you up top," Dorian announced.

Aleister smiled and replied, "As you wish."

In a matter of seconds the two men were off to Lady Darlington's mansion. Once there, they knocked on the door. Jack answered and acted as though he had just seen Doctor Wellington for the first time that night. Aleister assumed that Lucian was able to convince Frances not to mention Lucinda and the reason the body was found.

"Good morning. Chief Inspector Anderson sent for us. He said there has been a murder here last night," Inspector Archer said.

"Yes, he has been with Lady Darlington and myself asking questions. This way please," Jack said.

As he led them toward the stairs they met Chief Inspector Anderson at the foot of the staircase. Chief Inspector Anderson reached out to shake Doctor Wellington and Inspector Archer's hands.

"Aleister, thank you for coming. Inspector, this way."

Lucian led the men to the grounds behind the mansion. Inspector Archer was just as horrified as with the first murder. Aleister's appearance and reaction was convincing; he was surprised at how different the body of Rose looked in the predawn light than it had in the dark. The scene was much more vivid and disturbing even to him.

"Who found her? Do we have any new information that will help us?" Inspector Archer asked.

"Nothing new," Chief Inspector Anderson began and continued to explain everything— everything except Lucinda's vision.

"I would like to speak with Lady Darlington now if you have nothing further," Inspector Archer said.

"Of course," Chief Inspector Anderson and the three men walked into the house.

Lucian and Aleister went in and waited in the parlor for Dorian to speak with Frances.

Jack led Dorian to Frances' room. It pained Jack knowing that she had feelings for this man and he had feelings for her and that Jack had to be the one to take him to her room and leave them alone. Jack once again softly knocked on her door and called to her. When she gave permission to enter, Jack begrudgingly opened the door to let Inspector Archer into her bedroom.

"Should I stay?" Jack asked, knowing damn good and well what the answer would be.

"No. That will be all. Thank you, Jack," Frances said as she positioned herself in a sitting position. "Please, have a seat, Inspector," Frances said and gestured to the chair that Chief Inspector Anderson had been sitting in earlier.

"Thank you," he replied.

"I suppose you want to ask about Rose," Frances said.

"Yes. Actually I do. Can you tell me when you last saw her?" his questioning began.

Frances proceeded to answer his myriad of questions, many of which she had already answered for Chief Inspector Anderson. Then, when the police questions subsided, Inspector Archer softened and wanted to know how Frances was.

"Frances, I am so sorry about your servant. I am also sorry that I had to ask so many questions about the murder so coldly. Is there anything I can do for you?" Dorian's tone softened even more.

"I don't think so. I will be fine. It was just so sad. She was a very kind person. I don't know why anyone would want to hurt her. I don't know how someone could have done this." Frances' eyes began to tear up again. "Do you think the rest of us are safe here?"

"I cannot say. I would not have thought otherwise and yet this happened. If you would like, I can have a policeman placed here for a while for your protection," Dorian offered.

He shivered at the idea that the body of the dead woman on the grounds out back could have just as easily been Frances. He was never happy when someone was hurt, but this time he was relieved to find that Rose had been murdered. When he heard that there was a murder at Frances' home he was so fearful that it had been Frances.

"Actually, that would be very nice. I would feel

much better even if it were only for a few nights. However, I do have one request, if I may," Frances said.

"Of course anything. What is it you wish?" Dorian asked.

"Would you be the policeman who stays? I would feel so much safer if it were you."

"Well, I had not considered it to be me. But I don't see why that would be a problem. I will stay for at least a week and make certain that no one is harmed," Dorian agreed.

He was surprised by her request, but at the same time happy and flattered. He would love to spend more time with Frances. He had wanted to get to know her better. He had so enjoyed the night he had spent talking and laughing with her. He desperately wanted more time with her like that.

"Thank you so much. This means a great deal to me," Frances said.

"You are very welcome. I must go now; I have so much to do today regarding this murder. I will be back before the sun sets," Dorian promised.

"Then I will hold dinner for you. We shall dine together," Frances said.

"Thank you, but that is really not necessary."

"Of course it is. It is the least I can do. After all you are going to be here protecting me. So I will see you for dinner then," Frances said.

"Dinner then." Dorian smiled and left the room.

He took one final glance over his shoulder and was happy that she did not notice. He just had to have one last look at her to get him through the day. Dorian regrouped with Chief Inspector Anderson and Doctor Wellington downstairs.

They concluded and the body was sent back to Aleister's office. Aleister examined the body of Rose the servant and went home to Lucinda.

Chief Inspector Anderson, exhausted from the ordeal, went back to the station to write out his findings and then retired early that day.

Inspector Archer finished his paperwork and returned to dine with Frances.

Victoria took advantage of the early evening that Lucian took; he and her took a long walk and talked.

Jack cared for Frances. And Lucinda did as was requested and went to speak with Frances.

Chapter 16

Lucinda and Victoria were informed of everything that had happened. Doctor Wellington sent Lucinda to see Frances and he went to his office.

Lucinda's carriage pulled up in front of Frances' mansion. Lucinda had a feeling of gloom and dread come over her knowing that there had now been three deaths on that property that she knew of. How many more lives will this place claim?

She walked to the door and dropped the knocker three times in succession. She was surprised to be greeted by Frances. She hugged her friend immediately.

"Frances, I am so sorry. I know that you were close to Rose."

"Yes, I was. You are one the few whom know just how close I am with my staff. They are the closest thing to family that I have. I just feel terrible that she met her fate here under my care. I wish I could go back and change the past," Frances said.

"Aleister said you had some questions about the visions."

"Yes. How long have you had them and why did you have one of Rose's murder? Start from the beginning."

Frances ushered Lucinda into the parlor and pulled her down on the couch beside her.

"Well, it all started during the Jack the Ripper

murders. I had visions of the prostitutes being murdered. I had dreams of the murders at night while I was at Lady Kinsington's."

"Were your visions of no help to the police?"

"I only told Aleister, Sylvia, and Victoria. Lucian did not learn until later. There was no way I could help in the investigation. The visions occurred either during or post murder, so by the time I had awakened and was able to tell someone the victim was already dead."

"So is this what happened last night?" Frances asked.

"Yes. I dreamt of Rose being mutilated. She was already dead when the dream began. I stayed and watched the cloaked figure slice her with his blade. Not out of morbid curiosity, but in an attempt to catch a glimpse of the face. Alas, my attempt was futile. When the figure finally turned to face me, I saw nothing under the hood of the cloak. The figure appeared to be faceless. It was almost as though it was mocking me," Lucinda continued.

"Why do you have these visions? Do you think there is a connection? Do you think this is Jack the Ripper beginning his murder spree once again?"

"I am not sure why the connection. Maybe it has something to do with this house. On one of the first nights that I stayed here I saw a black figure here in this very room. I don't know if there was some kind of connection made at that point or not. I don't think this is the same person as before. I almost think that the thing that was in this house has found a new conduit for its bidding."

"What do you think this thing is?"

"I truly believe it is the necromancer— the doctor."

"Doctor Middleton, the original owner?"

"One in the same," Lucinda frankly declared.

"So why then and why now? What is the trigger for his murderous spree?"

"I believe that I triggered him the first time— my presence here. Aleister and Ms. Poe both said that there had never been such strong and frequent activity in the mansion until I arrived. And now, I think he has returned due to your activities and openness to the spiritual plane."

The conversation became too heavy for Frances, thinking that her actions may have released something that has caused so much pain and especially to Rose, her mood sobered. Frances now felt fear where before the thought of a spirit residing in her home excited and thrilled her.

"Well, I would like to leave this topic now," Frances said.

"Of course. It is not a pleasant one for me. It is not one that I wanted to explore in the first place. I knew that you needed to know what I knew. I would gladly like to change topics. Let's discuss Dorian Archer," Lucinda said.

Frances immediately smiled. "What would you like to say about Dorian Archer?"

"I would like to say that he is a very handsome man and I am certain that his taken with you. I would like to know what happened when he accompanied you on your carriage ride."

"Well, I can say he did not go home right away. He insisted on escorting me home safely and I invited him in.

He accepted and he stayed here until dawn. We talked and laughed all night. It was so nice. I have never known a man like him before. And he is going to stay here for at least a week to ensure my safety."

"Frances, I knew he would be the one to steal your heart. It's good that he will be here to protect you. You can get to know him while he is here."

As Lucinda was talking to Frances, she kept an uneasy feeling. She kept her guard up and was certain she was being watched. Even though she loved visiting Frances, she could not wait to leave that house. Finally it was time for her to get back home. She knew that Aleister would be getting home early and she wanted to be there before he arrived. So she bid Frances farewell and promised to check her in a few days.

Lucinda arrived home about an hour before Aleister. She thanked Ms. Poe for taking care of Elizabeth and she told her everything that had happened.

"Lucinda, is there anything I can do?" Ms. Poe asked as she patted Lucinda's hand.

"You already help so much. You are there for us and for Elizabeth. Thank you," Lucinda said.

"I will get Elizabeth for you and then I will get the evening meal prepared," Ms. Poe started to get up.

Lucinda took her hand and said, "I will get Elizabeth. You get the kitchen staff started on dinner and then you go rest. You have been up as long as I have."

"Oh dear, I am just fine. I will take care of things for you," Ms. Poe reassured.

"Really, Ms. Poe, I insist," Lucinda reiterated how important her request was to her.

"Very well. You get your sweet child and I will get the kitchen staff cooking."

Ms. Poe headed to the kitchen and Lucinda went to retrieve Elizabeth from the nursery where she was being cared for by one of the maids. She cuddled her daughter she had missed terribly. She rarely left her side and never for this length of time.

When Aleister arrived home, he found Lucinda in the nursery with their daughter. He stood in the doorway and admired what he had, Lucinda unaware that he was there at first.

"Aleister, you startled me. How long have you been standing there?" Lucinda playfully scolded.

"Only a minute or so. I just love watching you with Elizabeth," Aleister admitted.

"I find it strange."

"Find what strange?" Aleister asked as he walked on in the room and sat beside his wife and child.

Lucinda handed Elizabeth over to Aleister and said, "How you can sneak up on me and I cannot tell, however in that house I can feel that presence so heavy watching and looming over me the entire time I am there."

"I mean no harm to you so your guard is down. You know that whatever is in the house is menacing and your guard is up," he said as he smiled at his daughter and shook her hand as she grasped his finger.

"I suppose."

"I fear you being in that house for any length of time. I must say I had a strange sensation being back there today. I had not noticed the melancholy and dead feeling in that house before. It was quite unsettling," Aleister said.

"That it is. Did you finish your examination of the body?"

"Yes. I was able to give the corpse a semblance of the woman it once was. I know that Frances will want a funeral for her. What exactly did you and Frances discuss today?"

"Well, the conversation began about the dreams and I had to explain that to her. Then it turned to Dorian Archer. She is really smitten with him. He has offered to stay as protection for at least a week. Apparently he is much more taken with her than I originally thought. Something does concern me though." "Really. What might that be?" Aleister asked

"I love Frances to death and she is one of my dearest friends, but she had never been able to commit to one man and right now Dorian is not the only man in her life," Lucinda admitted to her husband.

"Is it Jack?" Aleister asked.

"Yes. How did you know?" Lucinda replied.

"I am not blind. He is very protective of her and she is overly kind to him. And then today I thought it strange that she allowed him into her bedroom. He took care of her as a husband would a wife and she allowed it. It was pretty obvious that there is some sort of relationship," Aleister responded.

"Do you think Dorian could tell?" Lucinda asked.

"Probably not. When Frances calmed down Jack wasn't as protective. And Dorian cannot see past his infatuation. So I don't think he noticed. But if he stays there for a week, it may become obvious to him."

"You do not think Jack would cause problems for her if he thinks she has found someone to replace him do you? Do you think Jack could be dangerous?"

"I don't believe so. He seems to genuinely care for Frances. He desperately wants to protect her, and I think that means letting her find a man that society deems is a suitable match for her," Aleister said.

Chapter 17

Broderick came home late again. He had been avoiding Lilly since their argument a few nights before. Each evening he had asked the staff if she had been abusive in any manner. Each evening their answer was no. And each evening when he returned home, Lilly wanted to talk about the argument, each evening he declined.

Then on fourth evening, Chief Inspector Anderson and Inspector Archer came to visit Broderick at work. He was surprised that they had not paid him a visit earlier. The murder of Lady Darlington's maid had spread fast. In fact, everyone in London had heard of the murder by that evening.

"Gentlemen. I don't think I need to ask why you are here, do I? It's about Lady Darlington's maid," Broderick said.

"Yes it is. I am very sorry to have to keep asking you to verify your whereabouts," Chief Inspector Anderson said. "I have known you for many years and I have known you to be a good man. I honestly think that things aren't as black and white as they seem. I think you were framed, but until we find the murderer we must question you about new cases. So may we have a few moments of your time?"

"Of course. I am a judge so I understand how it all works. To be honest, sometimes I wonder if I am innocent— of those three murders. I know I am of the rest. But that night I just can't recall anything past the drinks and starting up the stairs," Broderick said.

"Can anyone verify your whereabouts on the night Rose was murdered?" Inspector Archer asked.

"Yes. I was with Lilly. She has been staying with me since the night of the murders of three women I was with. We actually had an argument that night about her behavior with my staff," Broderick said.

"What about your staff?" Inspector Archer asked.

"Lilly became abusive to my maid. I came home and stopped her just before she struck my maid with a candlestick. We had an argument and haven't really spoken since. She has still been staying with me, but I have been working late to avoid conflict. In fact— well, I had been sharing a platonic bed with her but not since that night," Broderick admitted.

"So she could not say if you were home or not, and you cannot say if she was home or not?" Chief Inspector Anderson asked.

"I guess not," Broderick said.

"Maybe we should have a talk with Lilly as well," Chief Inspector Anderson said.

"You don't think Lilly is capable of murder?" Broderick asked.

"You said she was violent with your maid," Inspector Archer said.

"Yes, but I think she is just spoiled, not a murderer," Broderick said.

"Nevertheless, I think we need to speak with her," Chief Inspector Anderson said.

"Of course. I understand," Broderick replied.

They continued asking questions about his relationship with Lady Darlington, if he knew the maid, Rose, and a myriad of other questions pertaining to the murder. Then they thanked him for his time and excused themselves.

As soon as they were outside they began to speculate about Lilly Meriwether. They decided to go directly to Broderick's home and speak with Lilly.

When they arrived at Broderick's home and knocked on the door they were greeted by a maid.

"I am Chief Inspector Anderson and this is Inspector Archer. Is Ms. Meriwether here? We understand she has been staying here with Judge Smith."

"Well— um let me see if she is in. Could you please wait here?" she said as she closed the door on them.

They looked at each other in sheer astonishment; neither man had ever had a door closed in their face before, especially when conducting police business.

The maid returned and let them in. They could tell that the maid was embarrassed by her actions.

"This way please," she said as she led them into the parlor.

"Ms. Meriwether, thank you for seeing us. We apologize for intruding unannounced. We have a few questions for you if you don't mind," Inspector Archer said.

"I am surprised you haven't stopped by earlier to harass Broderick. I heard about Lady Darlington's maid.

Have you questioned her staff?"

"As a matter of fact, we did our job that night. And might I add we were very thorough. We have also been by to speak to Broderick and now we are here to speak with you," Chief Inspector Anderson said.

"So Broderick knows you are here?"

"Yes we asked his permission before we came," Inspector Archer said.

"We understand that you have been staying here since the triple murder," Chief Inspector Anderson said.

"That is correct. I thought Broderick needed the support."

"I also understand that you sleep in separate rooms," Inspector Archer said.

"I do not think that our sleeping arrangements are the concern of the police. Since when does sleeping arrangements between adults involve the police?" Lilly was becoming defensive and angry.

"We just need to establish whether there can be a concrete alibi for you and Broderick. If you are sleeping in separate rooms there is no way that each of you can say for sure that neither left the house on the night in question," Chief Inspector Anderson explained.

"That is offensive and preposterous. Are you now accusing me of murder?" Lilly demanded.

"Ms. Meriwether, there is no reason to become upset. We are not accusing anyone. We are still trying to eliminate people. So if Broderick could not have been there then he would be eliminated from that murder and would look less like a suspect in the others," Chief Inspector Anderson said.

"I thought he was already ruled out of an earlier attack. So why are you questioning his whereabouts again?" Lilly demanded.

"We would just like to check alibis for the most recent murder," Chief Inspector Anderson calmly replied.

"Gentlemen I am afraid I am going to have to ask you to leave now. I will contact my father's attorney and he will make arrangements to be with me when you ask your questions," Lilly said as she stood. She then abruptly turned and walked briskly from the room.

They sat there and looked at one another once again in disbelief. They heard Lilly's raised voice and then the maid who had let them in came back and ushered them out with tears in her eyes.

The two men could not believe the manner in which they were treated by Lilly. On their way back to the police station they discussed Lilly's odd behavior. This was very suspicious. Was she upset because she was protecting Broderick or herself, or was she just very upset because she was indeed spoiled and was offended because she had the perception of being treated like a suspect?

The two men returned to the police station and made note of Lilly Meriwether's behavior in their files. They read over their notes, what little witness statements there were, and the crime scene photos. Nothing really stood out— they were at a standstill in this investigation.

Several weeks passed and there were no further murders. London had calmed down and things had almost returned to normal.

Chapter 18

Dorian Archer had become extremely close to Lady Frances Darlington. They had their meals together, spent time walking and talking together. Frances dreaded the day when Dorian would tell her he thought she would be safe and he would return to his home. She held her breath every morning fearing those uttering of the words, "I must go now." Nevertheless it happened one morning at breakfast.

Frances came down to have her breakfast and Dorian was already seated awaiting her.

Dorian stood and greeted Frances when she entered the room, "Good morning, my lady. How did you fare last night?"

"I slept very well, and yourself?" Frances replied.

"I slept well," Dorian smiled then continued, "I think we need to discuss your safety."

The disappointment spread across her face and she asked, "What exactly about my safety would you like to discuss?"

"Well, it has been two weeks and there have been no further murders and everything appears to be all well here. I really need to get back to my home and tend to my personal affairs there. But if you should have problems be assured, I will be the first one here to care for you." Dorian tried to reassure her.

"I understand, however I would like for us to still

see one another. I have grown quite fond of you and I think we have become very close," Frances said as her eyes glazed over with tears.

Dorian had wanted to take her since the day he met her, and now knowing how badly she wanted him to stay let him know just how she felt— let him know that she felt for him the way he felt for her. He could no longer control his actions— he had held back too long, longer than he thought possible.

Dorian dropped his fork, pushed his chair back and rushed to Frances. He pulled her from her chair and kissed her passionately on the mouth. Frances had never before wanted anyone this badly as she returned the passion in his kiss.

Dorian lifted her in his arms as though she weighed no more that a delicate bird. He carried her to her bedroom and kicked the door shut behind him. He laid her gently on her oversized bed amongst the plush pillows that were scattered about. His lips left her mouth and trailed her neck to the top of her bodice, but that obstacle was short lived as he pulled and tugged at the ties until her bodice was loosened and her breasts were exposed.

Dorian stopped momentarily as if to give her time to object. He looked deeply into her eyes— so deeply that he became lost in them.

Frances placed her hands on either side of his face and pulled him into her breasts. She relished in his mouth exploring her bare nipples. She trembled beneath his touch as it grew more aggressive.

Dorian reached up under her dress and pulled her undergarments down, then loosened his trousers. He ran his hand slowly up her thigh and found a resting spot in the most of sacred of places. He once again looked in her eyes longingly as if to give her the chance to object— she did not. Dorian positioned himself and made entrance.

Frances arched her back and whimpered. She was by no means a virgin, but the experience with Dorian was a first. She had never loved the men she had been with— never loved them with her heart and soul. She had never loved a man enough to die for him. She knew she would give anything to Dorian— do anything for this man. As he continued his sweet assault on her she found euphoria.

Dorian grasped her wrists and held them above her head as he continued. Her sweet moans brought him to the brink; then she tensed one last time and sent him over the edge. He collapsed on her and breathed heavily of her lilac-scented silky hair.

Dorian knew he could deny her nothing now. If she asked him to stay, he must. He now belonged to her. He wanted nothing else but to be her puppet— puppet to dance on a string at her whim.

The young lovers did not have the privacy they had thought. Jack had passed by her bedroom. His heart had broken into a million shards. Deep in his heart he knew that he could never be with her the way he wanted. He knew that she did not love him in the way he wanted even though she had many times given herself to him and had a special relationship with him. He knew that one day someone would come along that she could be with— someone that she would love in that special way. It appeared that Dorian Archer was that man. It did not matter. Jack knew he could never leave her side; he would be there with her and for her until the day she took her last breath. He would be there to pick up the pieces if this man left her broken hearted. With tears in his eyes, he went on about his day— he would do as she wished.

Dorian readied himself for work as Frances lay there in bliss.

"I must really go in to work now. I am late, but I still must go," Dorian said as he smiled at her.

"I understand. When will I see you again?" Frances asked hopefully.

Dorian walked over to the bed and sat beside her. He took her hand and kissed it, then said, "Why, tonight of course."

Frances sat up and hugged him.

"That's wonderful," she said and then pulled back with a serious look on her face. "But for how long? How long will you stay here?"

"How long do you want me to stay here?" Dorian asked.

"Until the stars no longer shine," Frances said.

"Very well. I suppose I should pack my things and bring them here then." He smiled.

"Are you jesting with me?" Frances asked.

"I am not if you want me here forever, then here is where I am bound. I can be no other place but by your side. I have loved you since the day I first saw you. And I have loved you more each time I saw you. Living here the past two weeks without being with you has been pure torture," Dorian admitted. "I had to prolong my stay to be with you as long as possible even though I knew you were not in danger."

"It has been for me as well. Why did you decide that now was the time?" Frances asked.

"The look on your face when I said I was leaving told me everything you had been thinking— your fears and your immense love. How could I not take you knowing the love that was there?" Dorian replied.

He leaned over and kissed her again on the mouth, long and hard, passionate and loving. He pulled away slowly.

Dorian looked deeply into Frances' eyes and said, "I love you, Lady Frances Darlington. But I really need to be off for now."

He smiled and stood. He turned to walk away then stopped, pivoted on his heels and looked at her with a great smile on his face.

"However, before I go I would like to ask a question of you."

"What?" Frances asked.

"May I share your bed tonight?" Dorian asked.

"Tonight and every night there after," Frances replied.

Dorian smiled and left without another word.

*****

Broderick had still been avoiding Lilly. Though she was still staying with him they barely saw one another and barely spoke. He loved her deeply, but was terribly annoyed with her behavior and her constant provoking. He had been so thrilled when she stood by him after the triple murder, but then her behavior had become so dramatic and odd.

There was an air of darkness that had fallen about Broderick's home— about his life. Lilly had become like a dark cloud hanging over him. He was saddened by the way she was making him feel— by the way she was behaving. She was not the woman he had fallen in love with.

It had been approximately two weeks since Lady Darlington's maid had been murdered and Broderick wanted desperately to have the Lilly he fell in love back once again. He was determined to repair their relationship. He stopped and purchased roses and a bottle of the best wine the winery had. He arrived only to find that once again, Lilly was belittling the staff.

Lilly turned to see him standing in the foyer just outside the parlor. She had been taking out her anger over a broken dish on the maid.

Broderick asked in a loud thunderous voice that he did not recognize as his own, "What in the Hell is going on here!"

The poor maid immediately apologized and hunkered down in the floor on her knees. Broderick was appalled; his staff had never cowered in fear before. He gently reached down and took her by the hand and coaxed her to her feet.

"A broken dish? That's all?" he asked the maid.

"Yes, Sir. I am very sorry. Please take it from my pay," she answered with tears in her eyes.

"Have I ever reacted harshly to a broken dish?"

"No, Sir," the maid replied.

"Then why would I now? You go to bed," he said.

"But the evening meal... I have to cook," the maid replied.

"Not tonight. We will manage without you. If you are hungry later you can prepare yourself something. For now, go and rest," Broderick said.

The maid left the room in relief that her master was not a brute, but a kind man.

Broderick turned his attention to Lilly, "What is your problem? I have warned you not to treat my staff in a harsh or demeaning manner and yet you do. Apparently they are so fearful of you that they will not confide in me the brutality they have endured from you while I have been at work. This ends now," Broderick said.

"You are a weak man letting your staff run your house as they please! They need to be taught their place! I intend to do that. Do you think I am going to marry you and move in here with them behaving the way you allow them to?" Lilly yelled out.

"You will not. And if that is the way you intend to behave in my house, you can leave," Broderick said.

Lilly became irate and charged Broderick yelling, "You think you can throw me out? I am a Meriwether and my father will have your seat on the courts if he discovers the manner in which you treat me— your fiancé."

Lilly slapped Broderick and hit him in the chest several times. Broderick did not raise a hand to her. She turned to storm from the room but paused momentarily, then turned to face Broderick and declared that she was going nowhere.

Broderick could take no more. He threw the wine bottle at her feet and the roses in her face.

"You will leave— and leave this moment," he said as he took her by the arms and pulled her to the front door. He pushed her outside and closed the door in her face. "I will have your things brought to you first thing tomorrow by messenger. Consider the engagement called off. Feel free to keep the ring, but please do not grace my presence again," he said through the door.

Lilly beat away at the door for what seemed like an hour until she finally left.

Broderick felt a sense of relief he had not felt since about a week after the triple murders that he was an unofficial suspect in. Even that did not loom over him like living with Lilly. He was happy that she had moved in with him briefly; he was thankful that he discovered the person she truly was before he married her.

He turned and walked into the parlor to clean up the wine bottle and rose mess. He noticed someone walking to him.

The poor maid who had caught the brunt of Lilly's brutality came over and knelt down in front of Broderick. She began picking up the pieces of brown glass from the floor.

"Daisy, don't. This is my mess. I told you to rest," Broderick said.

"This is my job. I really don't mind," she replied.

He took the glass from her hand and dropped it. He held her hands in his and coaxed her to her feet.

"Daisy, I am so sorry. Why did you not tell me what she was doing?"

"She is your fiancé. It is not my place to question her authority or to carry tales and cause problems."

"She was my fiancé. The engagement has been called off. She had no authority here; she was merely a guest. I'm sorry; I should have made that clear to you. You do not have to worry about her anymore."

Daisy broke down in tears and fell into Broderick's arms. She cried so hard that she heaved and gasped for her breath.

Broderick's heart broke that he had let this sweet girl be tormented by a tyrant— a tyrant he thought was a saint. He felt so ashamed that he was led astray and tricked by such a cruel woman. He held Daisy and let her cry until she had calmed down.

"I'm sorry, Sir. I shouldn't have. I acted out of my place," she apologized.

"Out of place? What do you mean? You are person no less than I; I am definitely no better than you. You need not apologize for being human," he pulled her back to his chest and hugged her.

Daisy knew he was a kind man but was extremely surprised by his actions that night.

*****

Lilly was infuriated. She walked the streets for many hours before she went to her father's house. It was just before dawn when she went in and up to her room. She did not sleep; she merely changed clothes. She was awaiting breakfast so that she could tell her father of the events from the night before.

Judge Meriwether was shocked to see his daughter once again sitting at his table for breakfast.

"Lilly, what on earth are you doing here?" he asked.

"Broderick threw me out and broke off the engagement over a maid," she said.

"He is sleeping with a maid now?" her father asked, surprised.

"No! He defended her when I tried to punish her for breaking a dish," she yelled.

"Just a dish. Was there more? It doesn't seem like Broderick to get that upset over scolding the staff. What type of punishment were you implementing?" her father asked, afraid he knew the answer.

"There had been other occasions with this maid. He insists on treating them like family. I set forth my authority and Broderick called off the engagement and sent me away," she said in a raised voice.

"Lilly, darling, you can be a bit overbearing to the staff. We have discussed this here before. Just go to him and assure him you will treat his staff the way he expects," he said.

"I no longer want him. I want you to destroy him!" she demanded.

"Lilly, what are you saying? What do you propose I do? I am definitely not going to kill the man."

"Destroy his position as judge. Destroy his reputation," she demanded.

"Lilly, the man is an upstanding citizen and a well respected judge. Why do you think he has not been arrested for those murders? No one believes that he did it. I will not even attempt to destroy his position or reputation. You are going to have to deal with this on your own or just walk away from him."

"I will deal with it on my own. I will do what a man should do— a man with a spine, not a weak man," Lilly said as she stormed back to her room.

The cook came into the dining hall, "Is there anything you need, Sir?"

"No, thank you," the judge sighed.

She turned to walk away and looked back over her shoulder, "Is Miss Lilly back for good, Sir?"

"I'm afraid so— and it looks like she will be here for quite some time.

The cook turned and walked back into the kitchen with her head hung low.

*****

Lucian was awakened at dawn by a messenger knocking at his door— a messenger that had been sent by Dorian Archer. The note from the messenger read *Another murder in Whitechapel. Come quick. Will wait on you there.*

He went back to the bedroom to tell Victoria. He roused her gently.

"Victoria, there has been another murder. I must go now. I will be back home early this evening," Lucian said as he kissed her gently on the forehead.

Lucian changed his clothes, put on his shoes and left within minutes of receiving the message from Dorian. Victoria lay there silently in the dark for what seemed like hours; she could not sleep— these murders were weighing heavily upon her, reminding her of the terrible things that she had once done. She could see clearly now how wrong they were.

Morning came and Lucian was still gone. She decided to go to the police station and see who had fallen into the hands of the murderer. She readied herself and had breakfast. She instructed Marie what her plans were and left her son in the capable hands of her favorite maid. She called for the coachman and was driven to the station.

*****

Lucian went directly to Whitechapel where he found Dorian hovered over another unfortunate victim. Weary-eyed Dorian stood and greeted Lucian.

"Chief Inspector, thank you for coming out at this hour. This one was found by a poor vagrant. I know him; I bought him food and a room before. He came to my door as soon as he found her," Dorian explained.

"Did the man see anything that could help us identify the murderer?" Lucian asked.

"Nothing— well, I don't know if this is substantial, but we did find this lying beside the victim," Dorian said as he handed a small button to Lucian.

"A button? Did it come from the victim?" he asked.

"It's highly unlikely. This is a very expensive button. It is made of mother of pearl," Dorian explained.

"How do you know this?" Lucian asked.

"You know I have been staying with Lady Darlington. She has many expensive pieces of clothing with similar buttons. I thought they were very beautiful and unique. She explained what they were and that they were expensive," Dorian explained.

"So they are buttons from women's clothing?" Lucian asked.

"Not necessarily. These buttons are used on both women's clothing and men's clothing. I have seen Lucinda and Aleister Wellington wear buttons like these. I have also seen Lilly Meriwether and Broderick Smith wear similar buttons. I think I have even seen these type of buttons on your wife's dress the night of the dinner," Dorian said.

"So you are saying the only thing we know for certain is that this button came from someone of relative wealth. What is the likelihood that this came from the murderer and not just dropped?" Lucian asked.

"Think about it, Chief Inspector. What person of wealth would find their way in these back alleys? Would you come back here if it weren't absolutely necessary?" Dorian asked.

"I suppose not. So we have a problem. If the murderer is someone of wealth, they are probably someone of high status— someone of power," Lucian said as he ran his fingers through his hair in frustration.

Dorian watched Lucian pace as he waited on the Chief Inspector to have an epiphany. But nothing came.

"What should we do? Who should we look at as suspects? Maybe we should take a closer look at Broderick?" Dorian asked.

"What about Lady Darlington? One of her maids was murdered on her grounds; do you think...?" Lucian asked.

"Well, I— um, I know she wasn't out here last night," Dorian said.

"How can you be certain?" Lucian asked.

"I— I was with her all night. I was in bed with her all night. I know she never even stirred. Please be discrete with this knowledge," Dorian said.

"What you do on your time is your business. Lady Darlington is an adult. I hope you know that she will most likely tell Lucinda Wellington and my wife as soon as she sees them next; they are all close friends and keep no secrets from one another," Lucian said as he smiled.

"So, Frances has been officially ruled out. I think we should look more closely at Broderick and possibly Lilly Meriwether. We also need to look more closely into the staff at Frances' home," Dorian said.

"Okay. Let's finish up here and as soon as day breaks we will go to speak with Broderick Smith and Lilly Meriwether," Lucian said.

They worked diligently with the other policemen on the scene collecting the body parts of the victim and asking people who lived and worked in the area if they had seen or heard anything. They went back to the station and added the new paperwork with the other case files. They added these photographs to the others and at daybreak, they went to Judge Broderick Smith's home.

They knocked on the door several times until it was answered by Daisy.

"May we speak with the judge please? We have a few questions for him," Chief Inspector Anderson asked.

"Yes, of course. Come in. I will have to wake him," Daisy replied and walked off to retrieve Broderick.

Broderick appeared within minutes of Daisy's disappearance.

"Gentleman it is a bit early to receive visitors. Is this yet another inquisition pertaining to another murder?" Broderick asked.

"Yes. There has been another murder. You have to know that you appear suspicious because of such an assumption— and to actually ask us that question," Inspector Archer replied.

"Once again can you verify you whereabouts last night?" Chief Inspector Anderson asked.

"Yes. I was here. I was speaking with and comforting my maid, Daisy, here. She had a very trying day. We talked until around 3 AM," Broderick answered.

"Miss, can you say this is true?" Inspector Archer asked.

"Yes. It is true," Daisy replied and nodded her head.

"And what of Miss Meriwether? I assume she is still staying here with you. May we speak to her?" Chief Inspector Anderson asked.

"Actually, she is not staying here any longer. That is why my maid was upset. You see, I called off the engagement and sent Lilly back to her father's house because she was being abusive to my staff, especially Daisy. So I cannot say where Lilly was last night, or is this morning," Broderick answered.

"Can you tell us if you recognize this button?" Inspector Archer asked as he pulled the mother of pearl button from his pocket.

"I have seen buttons made of mother of pearl before. In fact, I have shirts adorned with them but none like this. It does look familiar, but I cannot say for sure who wore it. I am sorry," Broderick replied.

"Would you mind if we looked at your clothing?" the Chief Inspector asked.

"Not at all. I have nothing to hide. This way," Broderick said.

Broderick took them to his bedroom and showed them his clothing. Just as Broderick had said, there was not one piece of clothing with that particular button.

"Thank you, Broderick. I am so sorry to put you through this so many times, but..." the Chief Inspector said.

"It is very frustrating to me, but I do understand. Who was she?" Broderick asked.

"We have not been able to identify her yet," Inspector Archer replied.

Chief Inspector Anderson and Inspector Archer thanked Broderick again and bid him farewell. They left and went to the Meriwether house. This was one visit they were not looking forward to.

They arrived at the Meriwether's house and reluctantly knocked on the door. A maid greeted them. They explained who they were and why they were there.

"I will see if Ms. Meriwether is available. Please wait here," the maid said and walked away.

Judge Meriwether came in and greeted the two men.

"Gentlemen, what is this about? Why do you need to speak with Lilly?" the judge asked.

"There was a murder last night and we were wondering if she could tell us where she was," Inspector Archer said.

"Gentlemen, surely she is not a suspect," the judge said.

"She has been Broderick Smith's alibi for most of the murders, but the last one we questioned them about she could not be his alibi. We just want to speak to her. She is not an official suspect. Basically, we just wanted to know when she saw Broderick last. May we speak with her?" Chief Inspector Anderson asked.

Judge Meriwether instructed the maid to bring his daughter downstairs. Within minutes a disheveled and half-awake Lilly entered the room with a distained look on her face.

"I was sleeping. This could not wait until after lunch?" she snapped at the Chief Inspector and the Inspector, as well as her father.

"Lilly, we need to ask where you were last night

and who you were with," Inspector Anderson said.

"I was here all night. Now may I go back to bed?" Lilly snapped.

"What time did you retire and what time did you see the last person before you retired?" the Chief Inspector asked.

"This sounds like you think Lilly was involved. I think that will be all gentlemen. I would ask that you leave us now," Judge Meriwether said as he pointed to the door.

"Thank you for your time," Chief Inspector Anderson said.

The two men saw themselves out and headed toward the station. They discussed the odd behavior of Judge and Lilly Meriwether.

"Did you notice that Lilly and the judge both had mother of pearl buttons on their clothing?" Inspector Anderson asked.

"Yes. But as you pointed out, it is not uncommon for people of their wealth to wear buttons made of mother of pearl. However, I think it is odd that the judge would not allow us to question Lilly further and Lilly being so defensive," Chief Inspector Anderson said.

"I know that you said Frances was with you all night, but what about her staff? Do any of them act out of the ordinary?" Chief Inspector Anderson asked.

"No. Well— Jack is very protective of Frances to the point of being possessive at times. I know that they are close, but not sure exactly what their relationship is. It is at times unnerving. I feel as though I must compete for her attention when it comes to him. Her other employees seem fine," Inspector Archer replied.

"Maybe we need to go by and question Jack," Chief Inspector Anderson said.

"You don't think Jack is..." Inspector Archer asked.

"No one is immune from suspicion, really. Maybe he is not a murderer, but he may know who is or he may have seen something out of the ordinary. I really do not think the button belongs to him— Hell the button may not even belong to the murderer," Chief Inspector Anderson said, becoming frustrated.

"Very well. Let's call on Frances," Inspector Anderson said.

They took the carriage to Lady Frances' mansion. Dorian felt strange knocking on the door of the home he had been staying in for the past two weeks.

A maid that Dorian had become familiar with answered the door. "Inspector, why are you knocking?"

"We are here on a police business. Would you call Lady Darlington for us?" Dorian asked politely.

"Of course. Have a seat in the parlor. I will fetch her," the maid said as she disappeared from view.

It was only a matter of minutes before Frances greeted the two men.

"Well, this is a surprise. I did not expect Dorian until tonight and I did not expect to have you both come by as Inspector and Chief Inspector. So what is it?" she asked as she sat and gestured for them to sit across from her.

"Frances, there was another murder and this morning we found something near the victim. We are not sure if even belongs to the murderer or not, but nevertheless here it is," Lucian said as he pulled the button from his pocket and outstretched his hand.

"A button— and an expensive button at that. This was with the victim?" Frances asked as she reached out and took it from his hand.

"Do you recognize it? We thought you may have seen someone wearing it on a piece of clothing." Chief Inspector Anderson asked.

"Well, actually it is a very common button. In fact, I think I have clothing with this button on it. I'm sorry, I know I have seen these buttons on others' clothing, but I can't say for certain who," Frances said.

"Thank you. What about your staff? Has any been behaving strangely? Do any of them seem out of sorts? I'm so sorry to ask again, but we are getting desperate to find this fiend," Chief Inspector Anderson said.

"I understand. I will help in any manner that I can. As far as strange behavior in my staff, I have not noticed anything really. Well…" Frances trailed off and bowed her head slightly.

For the first time in her life she cared what someone thought of her. And she had not mentioned her relationship with Jack to Dorian yet. She honestly did not know how. Finally her long pause and obvious discomfort prompted a question by Chief Inspector Anderson.

"Frances, what is it? You can tell us. We will help you," the Chief Inspector said.

"It's actually something very personal. It is something I really need to tell Dorian first— something I should have told him sooner. Can I have a few moments alone with him?" Frances begged.

"Of course. I will step into the gardens. That was always my favorite spot here. Send a maid for me when you are ready," Chief Inspector Anderson said.

Frances could see the concern on Dorian's face and it worried her. She was sure that she was about to lose him.

"Frances, what is it?" Dorian asked.

"Dorian, please don't judge me too harshly. I have been alone most of my life. I have had my staff and my money, but I have answered to no one. Now I care about what one person thinks about my actions. I care about what you think. I do not want to lose you," Frances began.

"Frances, you are frightening me. What have you done?" Dorian pleaded as he took her by the hands.

"My life is a lonely one— up until recently. I, like everyone else in this cold world, needs companionship. Jack— Jack has been there for me. In more ways than one, if you know what I mean," Frances said as her eyes filled with tears.

Dorian dropped her hands and stood. He paced the room and ran his hands through his hair in frustration.

Frances stood and walked to him. She took hold of his arm. "Dorian, this was before we became intimate. Since then I have not been with Jack. Our relationship is understood. He is there when I need him only," she tried to explain.

"Frances, I don't know what I am supposed to say or how to react to this."

"I don't know either. I guess that's why I have been hesitant about telling you. You had to have known that I have been with others, my reputation proceeds me a bit, does it not?"

"I did know that there had been others before, just not a man who lives with you. I understand why he seems so protective of you. You have to know that he is in love with you. Do you not care about that? You just discard him when he is of no use? I cannot believe you can be so cold," Dorian said.

Frances was hurt by his perception of her, but it was accurate. She had a realization that what hurt more than how he perceived her was that her eyes were now open to what a horrible person she had been. She felt terrible that she had used Jack like she had and that now Dorian knew what a terrible wretch she was.

"I have no excuse. What you say is true. I never thought there would be another. I thought that I would be alone. Jack was there. I knew he was in love with me, but only discovered this recently. After the night you stayed here after the dinner party. He confided in me then. He was worried that you would hurt me. How ironic, you did not hurt me, but I have not only hurt you but him as well. All I can say is that I am sorry and that my relationship with Jack is over," Frances continued.

In the middle of the conversation Jack came to the entrance of the door and asked, "Is everything all right? Do you need anything?"

Dorian just looked at Frances with sadness and disappointment in his eyes.

"I am fine. We don't need anything. Thank you," Frances said.

Jack turned to leave but was halted by Dorian's voice.

"Frances has just confided in me about your relationship,"

Jack turned and asked, "And?"

"And do you have anything to add?" Dorian asked.

"I do not. I am her employee. If she requires more from me than my regular staff duties, I will oblige. That is it," Jack said.

"Are you in love with her?" Dorian asked.

"Is this question from an inspector or a lover?" Jack asked.

"I need to know as— well, not as an inspector," Dorian said.

"I fell in love with her the day I met her. The relationship was a wonderful surprise. But I have known all along that she was not in love with me. I know she loves me as a special friend, maybe more, but not as a man she wants to spend her life with. I was disappointed when I discovered her feelings for you, but not surprised. I knew this day would come eventually. She denied it, but I did not. If she has given her love to you, you would be a fool to throw it away because of a servant," Jack said.

Dorian did not reply and Frances could not believe her ears. Jack was giving her to Dorian.

"If that is all, may I continue my work?" Jack

asked.

Dorian stuttered, "Y-Yes. Thank you."

Dorian was silent. Frances could take the silence no longer. She had to know his thoughts.

"Dorian, you must tell me. Are you leaving me?"

Dorian turned with tears in his eyes and grabbed her by the arms. He pulled her closely and kissed her. Then he held her tightly.

Dorian whispered in her ear, "I could not if I wanted to. Are there any more secrets I should know of?"

"No. And I swear never to keep anything else from you," Frances cried.

"Now what of the strange behavior you needed to tell us about?"

"I have noticed Jack being more protective of me. I assume it was because of the murder on the grounds. But he has continued to be protective even while you have been here. I have noticed that a few times he has been on the grounds where the murder took place late at night, just standing and staring," Frances said.

"May we speak to him about that?" Dorian asked.

"Of course. I will send someone out to fetch Chief Inspector Anderson and Jack," Frances said.

She walked into the hallway and called out for one of her maids and instructed her to send in both the Chief Inspector and Jack. The maid returned in minutes with both men.

"I thought I had answered all of your questions," Jack said as he entered the parlor.

"This is not about the earlier discussion. This is about something else," Dorian said.

"Can you enlighten me on what is going on?" Chief Inspector Anderson asked.

Frances began, "I had to inform Dorian of a relationship that I had with Jack— an intimate relationship so that I could tell him that Jack had been behaving a bit strange."

Jack looked hurt and betrayed as he asked, "What strange behavior? I have been by your side making certain that you were safe, you call that strange behavior?"

"Jack, please do not be upset. I saw you a few nights during the night standing over the spot where Rose was found," Frances said.

Jack burst into tears and wept openly, "I was in love with Rose. We were going to tell you. I had been in love with you for years. But Rose and I became close and I thought you needed me— we thought you needed me. We wanted to ensure your happiness. Inspector Archer showed up in your life and I felt relieved because even though I loved you, I loved her more and I could tell you the truth about Rose and I. Then she was murdered. I was afraid to tell you after she was murdered. I was afraid that I would be accused. If you thought I was still in love with you, there would be no reason to think that there was anything between Rose and myself," Jack confessed. "I have been grieving at night where she took her last breath."

"Oh, Jack. I am so sorry. I wish you had told me sooner. I would have been happy for you and Rose,"

Frances said and embraced Jack.

"I'm sorry, Chief Inspector, I thought we had something," Dorian apologized.

"I think this is a discussion to be left here— better forgotten by myself. Dorian, I will see my way out and back to the police station. You should stay here and spend some time with Frances. I will see you tomorrow," Chief Inspector Anderson said.

"Thank you, Chief Inspector. I appreciate that," Dorian said as he shook hands with his mentor.

Chapter 19

Lucian went back to the police station and safely tucked the mother of pearl button in his desk drawer beside his corked half drank bottle of rum. He then returned to his home and to his Victoria.

Victoria jumped into Lucian's arms before he could even remove his frock coat.

"Oh, darling, I have missed you so today. You are home much earlier than I expected. Is everything alright? You look troubled," Victoria asked.

"I have discovered way too much about Dorian and Frances. Something I choose not to discuss. But you should see your friend tomorrow. She may need to seek your comfort and advice," Lucian said with a sigh.

"Is she alright? Has something happened to her?" Victoria pleaded with her husband to tell her more.

"It is relationship issues. Please do not make me say more," Lucian smiled.

"Oh, you tease me so. Just know that I will be tortured until tomorrow morning when I see her. As you wish. What shall we discuss?" Victoria asked.

"To begin with, why are you in such an uplifted mood?"

"Your son took his first step this morning. Come see for yourself," Victoria said as she pulled his hand, leading him to the nursery.

This was welcomed news to Lucian— something positive in a sad time with his work. He took his son from the maid, set him down on his feet, and pulled one hand, then the other until his son was steadying himself on his own.

"Come to father," Lucian said as he held out his hands close to his son in order to catch him should he fall.

His precious son took first one slow and unsteady step and then another and then another until he was in Lucian's arms. Lucian hugged him tightly and kissed his head.

"Oh, my boy, you can walk. I am so proud of you," Lucian said.

He and Victoria enjoyed their son for several hours and then the three of them had their evening meal. Lucian had such a wonderful time with his family, forgetting all of the horror and problems that lay outside his door.

That night he slept soundly beside his wife, more soundly than he had since their wedding night. He felt revived and carefree— like the tide was about to change. That night he slept more soundly than he had since their wedding night. Someone came up behind him and laid their hand on his shoulder.

This mysterious person said, "Do not turn; you do not need to see my face, nor know who I am. Just listen closely. You will put an end to these murders and you will do it tomorrow. You have already met the murderer, in fact, you know them quite well. In your heart you already know who this fiend is. Follow your heart and follow the scent of lilac and the sound of a sweet hummingbird. When you hear the tiny sound of *clipity clop* you will know you are close. Make haste and follow your senses."

Lucian awoke with a strange calm over him. He was refreshed and ready to face the day. He thought about the dream long and hard. He hoped and prayed that the prophetic dream would come to fruition that day. He went into work early and worked all day. But nothing— he had heard no hummingbird or *clipity clop*, nor did he ever once catch the scent of lilac.

Lucian and Dorian worked on the case and stayed late. Before they left, Lucian finally confided in Dorian about the dream.

"I know about Frances and her involvement and interest in spiritualism, but what are your thoughts? Do you think that the dream was just wishful thinking or prophetic?" Lucian asked Dorian.

"I have not mentioned this to anyone, not even Frances, but I have seen and heard some very strange things in that house. I have heard scratching and a disembodied voice calling my name. I have seen a faceless shadow figure lurking the halls at night. So I think a prophetic dream is highly likely," Dorian replied.

"Well, at any rate I must be getting home. It is already close to midnight. I will speak with you in the morning. Goodnight," Lucian said.

"Goodnight, my friend. Take care on your way home, for you may encounter the Ripper," Dorian said.

The two men left the police station and parted ways. Dorian took a carriage to Frances' home. Lucian was climbing into his carriage when he heard the sound that instantly caught his attention— it sounded like a horse trotting— *clipity clop, clipity clop*. He looked around but saw no one and the sound was so faint that he scarcely was sure he had heard it. Had it not been for his dream he would have paid no attention to it.

He walked toward the fleeting sound. He caught the faint scent of lilac and shivers went down his spine. He could not believe what he was encountering. He now followed the scent of lilac as well as the sound of a horse trotting. As he came closer to the trotting sound, he heard the sound of a woman humming— it sounded almost like the sound of a delicate bird singing.

Lucian's heart quickened as he hastened his pace. He had been so engrossed in the prophecy of his dream seemingly coming true, that he almost screamed when a hand fell upon his shoulder that stopped him dead in his tracks.

"Dorian, you gave me a terrible fright," Lucian whispered. "What are you doing?"

"When my carriage was a bit away from you, I noticed that you still had not started home. I was concerned when I looked to see you hastily headed in the opposite direction. I pulled my carriage back to the police station and followed you on foot from there. What are you doing?" Dorian asked.

"We must hurry. I heard the trotting of a horse and smelled the scent of lilac. Then just before you came up behind me I heard a sweet voice that sounded like a bird humming. Listen," Lucian whispered.

Dorian strained his ears and listened intently. He heard the humming and he smelled the lilac. "I hear it and I smell the lilac. This way!" He pulled Lucian by the arm in the direction of the humming.

Both men hastened toward the humming but it stopped. They stopped and listened, but now all they heard were hushed voices in the alley just beyond Broderick Smith's home. They crept toward the voices and could not believe their eyes, they saw a cloaked figure standing beside a woman. The figure was a woman they both knew. It appeared as if the woman had been forced to come along with the cloaked figure. She was sobbing and begging to be spared. They watched as the cloaked figure pulled something from under the cloak that shimmered in the moonlight, a knife.

The two men ran and took down the cloaked figure. They wrestled the knife from the figure. When they pulled back the hood they were astonished.

"Lilly Meriwether, you are under arrest for assault and attempted murder of Daisy," Inspector Archer said.

They lifted Lilly from the ground and handcuffed her and as they did Lucian, noticed something amazing. She was missing a button— a mother of pearl button— from the sleeve of her blouse. He pointed this out to Dorian.

"Lilly Meriwether, you are also under arrest in the recent Ripper murders," Dorian said.

They took Daisy home and explained that they would be back shortly to get a statement from Daisy. Then they took Lilly to the police station where they put her in a cold jail cell.

They went back to Broderick's home and asked Daisy to tell then what had happened.

She began by saying, "I heard a knock at the door. It was Ms. Meriwether. I asked her if I should wake Judge Smith and she said no that she had come for me. She brandished a knife and told me if I did not come with her she would gut me there in the doorway. I feared for my life. I did not know what else to do so I left with her. She grabbed my arms with such force, had I not known it was her I would have surely thought it was a man by the brute force and strength in which she handled me. She pulled me down to the alley and told me I would die like all the rest. I would die for causing Judge Smith to call off the engagement. Then you came," she sniffled.

"I think that is all that we need from you, Daisy. I am so sorry for your ordeal, I am just happy that we found you in time," Chief Inspector Anderson said as he put his hand on hers.

"I am so thankful to you both. Not only did you save my dear Daisy, but you also cleared my name in the process," Broderick said to the Chief Inspector and the Inspector. "But why did she do this and why did she want Daisy dead?"

"We are not certain. We are going to question her first thing in the morning," Chief Inspector Anderson said.

*****

Lilly sat in anger for hours. Thinking— thinking about how she came to be in this place. It was all Broderick's fault. If only he had been faithful and honorable. But no he had to sleep with every whore around, including trying to have his way with that stupid maid at Lady Darlington's home. Well, she took care of that before he could have that stupid maid, Rose. And it was added pleasure that she was Frances' favorite.

Lilly had been at odds with Frances for years, ever since the night that Frances bedded a man that Lilly had her eye on. The man was Samuel Jones and he was an immensely wealthy man. Frances had done like she always had, she had used him up and thrown him away.

Of the other whores whom she had rid London of, Broderick had slept with them all and not even bothered to be discrete in any manner. He was making her look like a fool. She had only wanted him to be faithful. When she saw how Broderick had defended that damned maid, Daisy, she knew that he was either sleeping with her or he was eventually going to.

Lilly hated them all. She would have done Lucinda and Victoria in as well had they not been so guarded by their husbands. Her biggest regret was that she could not cut the throat of Lady Frances Darlington and cut her into shreds, but that would have been impossible with the police inspector sleeping at her side. Really, did Frances think she was being discrete? Did she think that the entire community of London did not know that she was now lying with him?

Lilly thought about how wonderful it felt to slice through the flesh of all of the whores that Broderick had slept with. She remembered how wonderful the feeling of the blade penetrating and the gliding through the filthy flesh of the lowest of the sub-humans was. The sound of the flesh opening up as she worked her magic was music to her ears. The last gurgling sounds of the whores gasping for that last breath as the blood oozed from their throat was amazing to Lilly. And best of all to her was watching them writhe in pain, desperately clinging to the last bit of life.

Lilly thought to herself. *Just think, this would not have been possible if I had not gone to Frances' damned dinner party almost a year ago. Something happened that night. When I entered the garden something came over me— a moment of pure clarity. Clarity on how to take care of Broderick and his whores— kill the whores and implicate Broderick. They could never prove that he did it, but maybe it would scare him into monogamy. And it did work— until the incident with that fucking maid. Something came over her— something gave her the courage to do what needed to be done.*

Now it was over. She had been found out and had lost Broderick. The bitch friends all had their happy lives with their men and for Lucinda and Victoria their children. Lilly knew that this would never be the life for her. There was nothing left to do except one thing— end it all.

In one last desperate act of showing that she was still in control. Lilly pulled off her boots and unlaced them. She then tied her boots strings together and made a noose from them. She stood on the bed in the jail cell, stretched up on her tiptoes and tossed the boot string noose across one of the rafters. She slipped it over her head and pulled it tight. With one fell swoop she tipped the bed and was left hanging, her legs swaying back and forth until they came to a resting stop.

*****

Lucian returned home to tell Victoria that they had found the Ripper copycat. There was nothing to worry about anymore. No one would be looking into the murders so their secret was safe. The murderer was off the streets so everyone was safe.

"Oh my God, Lucian, why on earth would Lilly Meriwether do such a thing? How on earth did you catch her? Are you sure that she is the murderer?" Victoria asked.

"I'm not sure why she did it, but I am sure it was her that did it. We will be finding that out in the morning when I return to the police station. For now, I would like to rest. I would like to sleep soundly in the bed holding my wife knowing that there will be no new murders to investigate when I awake," Lucian said.

He held his wife tightly and kissed her deeply. He took her by the hand and led her to bed. In the morning Lucian arose early and went in to work. He wanted to tie up this investigation and take a few days off with his family.

*****

Dorian went back to Frances' mansion and explained everything to her. Her reaction was very similar to Victoria's. She was astounded; she knew Lilly had always been spoiled and snooty, but to have committed these macabre murders was totally unbelievable.

"Why? Did she say why she did it?" Frances asked. "Oh my God, Rose, why did she do that to Rose? Rose was not a prostitute. Rose was my favorite, she was a dear friend," Frances began to cry.

The night of Rose's murder all came flooding back to Frances. She was devastated to know that someone she had let into her house had come back and killed one of the few people whom Frances loved. She was inconsolable. Dorian held her and tried to comfort her. It was hours before she could gain complete composure.

Jack could tell from the solace in their conversation that it must be troubling and something that didn't need to be interrupted. When Frances had calmed herself, she and Dorian decided that Jack should know who murdered Rose. Frances called to him and as usual he came right away to see what she required of him.

Frances and Dorian explained to Jack that Lilly had been the murderer. Jack fell to the floor in a heap. Frances comforted him just as Dorian had comforted her earlier.

Dorian sat on the couch thinking how terrible this must be for Jack. He could not imagine loosing Frances in that manner and then to find out who had murdered her had been welcomed in that house and Frances had been a gracious host to her and the staff had all been kind to her. He felt helpless as he watched his beloved and her dear friend grieving for a second time over the loss of a close friend and lover.

*****

The next morning Lucian and Victoria went to see Aleister and Lucinda first thing. They explained everything that had happened the night before.

Aleister and Lucinda were stunned. They could not believe that Lilly had been the Ripper copycat. They bombarded Lucian and Victoria with questions.

They answered what they could and said they would explain everything once they spoke with Lilly and learned more.

Lucinda and Aleister saw their friends off. Lucian took Victoria home and headed to the police station. Little did Chief Inspector Lucian Anderson know what he was about to find at the station. Little did any of them know that they would never get answers from Lilly.

Ronda L. Caudill grew up in the small rural town in VA and married her high school sweetheart. They have been happily married for 25 years and have two wonderful daughters. Ronda earned her Ph.D. in Education from Capella University. She is the author of Birthright (A Nobleman Novel), The Choice (A Nobleman Novel), Forbidden Fruit, Ravenshire, The Forgotten (The Glass House Children of Ravenshire), and short stories A Night at the Bishop House and The Music Box Murders.